"Oh, God, Evie," Jess cried.

Eve followed Jess's transfixed gaze . . . The demon. There was something wrong about its gait. When Eve realized why the creature was moving in such an unnatural way it felt like a punch to the solar plexus. It had huge claws, blade-sharp claws shaped like scythes on all four feet . . .

Eve saw that the claws weren't the only atrocity. Like Jess had said, the demon had a face that was almost human, but warped, with a nose that was nearly non-existent. Against the sides of its head were the pointed ears of a bat. Its small eyes glowed red and held an intelligence that took Eve's breath away. It grinned, revealing insanely long, sharp teeth of a rotted-looking dingy yellow. It was enjoying itself.

The creature brayed again, white foam flying from its lips, then it stopped and tilted its head back, sniffing. *Did it just realize we're here?* Eve wondered.

Also available:

Dark Touch: Shadows

A Dark Touch Novel

THE HUNT

Amy Meredith

RED FOX

With special thanks to Laura Burns and Melinda Metz

DARK TOUCH: THE HUNT
A RED FOX BOOK 978 1 849 41052 6

First published in Great Britain by Red Fox,
an imprint of Random House Children's Books
A Random House Group Company

This edition published 2010

1 3 5 7 9 10 8 6 4 2

Series created and developed by Amber Caravéo

Copyright © Random House Children's Books, 2010

All rights reserved. No part of this publication may be reproduced, stored in a retrieval system, or transmitted in any form or by any means, electronic, mechanical, photocopying, recording or otherwise, without the prior permission of the publishers.

The Random House Group Limited makes every effort to ensure that the papers used in its books are made from trees that have been legally sourced from well-managed and credibly certified forests. Our paper procurement policy can be found at www.rbooks.co.uk/environment

Set in 12.25/16pt Minion by Falcon Oast Graphic Art Ltd.

Red Fox Books are published by Random House Children's Books,
61–63 Uxbridge Road, London W5 5SA

www.**kids**at**randomhouse**.co.uk
www.**rbooks**.co.uk

Addresses for companies within The Random House Group Limited
can be found at: www.randomhouse.co.uk/offices.htm

THE RANDOM HOUSE GROUP Limited Reg. No. 954009

A CIP catalogue record for this book is available from the British Library.

Printed and bound in Great Britain by
CPI Bookmarque, Croydon, CR0 4TD

For Carrie Enders, kickass chick

WAKEFIELD LIBRARIES & INFO. SERVICES	
30000010205630	
Bertrams	02/04/2012
VAM	£5.99

Prologue

'Dude, have you decided to give up showering?' Dave Perry called after practice on Monday. 'As the guy who sits behind you in history, let me say – bad idea.'

Kyle Rakoff laughed, veering away from the Deepdene High gym, where the rest of the football team was headed.

'Jogging home. Showering there,' Kyle shouted back. He turned, trotting backwards so he could continue the conversation. 'Then hitting Big Ola's. Sorry, Dave. I know how much you love sneaking a peek at my naked gloriousness.'

Dave gave an exaggerated fake laugh before disappearing into the gym. Kyle grinned, then turned round and picked up his pace a little. His muscles protested – practice had been killer today – but it also felt kinda good, running across the quad. His whole body was warm and purring like a Lamborghini.

Maybe he'd end up making it to Ola's before Helena did. She had to go in for algebra tutoring this afternoon. She needed it. If she didn't watch out, she'd be pulling a D for the semester. Kyle grinned, indulging in a little fantasy. So Helena would be late. And maybe that new girl – Brynn? Brenda? He was pretty sure it was something starting with B – would be there. Somebody must have clued her in that the ice-cream place on Main Street was where pretty much everyone from school hung out. He could get a little groundwork laid down. Maybe he'd even offer to show B-something around. Nothing wrong with being friendly.

Helena was great and all, but Kyle would not describe himself as monogamous – not that he'd ever done the deed with even one girl. But in theory. And B-something was a complete cutie with her super-short hair and her long, long legs. Or maybe Eve Evergold would be at Ola's. He needed a little more flirt time with her. Sure, she'd turned him down for coffee a few times, but she wouldn't be able to resist him for ever. Someday, someday not too far away, he knew he'd be running his hands through that long, dark hair of hers, seeing her dark blue eyes light up when she saw him.

Kyle decided to cut through the woods. He veered off the sidewalk and onto one of the narrow, twisting paths. His feet made crunching sounds on the fallen leaves that smothered the forest floor. This route would get him to his house probably five minutes sooner. And he could shower fast. Yeah, he should definitely make it to Ola's before Helena.

The branch of a fir tree slapped Kyle's shoulder. The trees were closer together than he remembered, maybe because the last time he'd taken this short cut he'd been about ten, with a lot less muscle and height on him. He should do it more often. The salty ocean air mixed with the earthy smell of the woods in a good way, and it was cool and dim and quiet. Kyle wasn't usually into quiet, but he'd left his iPod in his locker, and the quiet was sort of nice. Maybe he'd scout around a little sometime, see if there was a private place out here that was girl-romantic. Usually he made a bonfire down on the beach, but switching it up was . . .

A rustling sound in the brush off to his left pulled him away from his thoughts. *Probably a fox*, he decided. There were lots of them around. His mom even left bits of chicken out for them sometimes. She liked to sit out on the second-storey deck and look at them. She called it Fox Watch, and it usually involved cocktails. His dad liked the being-out-on-the-deck part and the cocktail part, but he hated that Kyle's mother fed the foxes. He called them vermin. Kyle's mom called them vermin too – red, pointy-eared, adorable little vermin.

Kyle felt a wave of pinpricks move across his shoulders. It felt like someone was watching him. And not a fox. He slowed down a little, glancing from side to side. He didn't see anything, but he heard the rustling sound again. Louder this time. A fox wouldn't shake the brush hard enough to make that sound. Would it?

Maybe they travel in pairs, he thought. At Fox Watch they definitely came a few at a time, but Kyle wasn't sure how big a part the chicken played in that.

He kept jogging – actually it was getting closer to running – but the feeling of being watched stayed with him. He suddenly remembered why he hadn't taken this route in so long. These woods had creeped him out when he was a kid. The last time he'd been through here, when he was little, he'd let his imagination run away with him completely. He'd been sure that the bogeyman was right on his heels.

And even though he was six years older – and a lot

bigger – it was happening again. He was giving himself the wiggins. *Man up*, he told himself, even though the prickly feeling was getting worse. The sensation wasn't just across his shoulders now. It was all the way down his back.

It was probably just because he'd been working out so hard at practice, really sweating, and now the sweat was drying, giving him chills. The theory worked – except for the fact that Kyle was running. His muscles felt hot, and fresh sweat was running down his face and back. His pits were pumping it out.

A strange sound came from behind him, a mixture of a bark and a howl. Foxes barked. He'd heard them. But he'd never heard a sound like that before. And the weird cry sounded like it came from something bigger than a fox.

'OK, fine, I'm a wuss,' Kyle muttered as he began to run full out, pushing himself as hard as he could.

Bad move. It seemed as if the fox – or whatever it was – could smell his fear, and Kyle's increased speed seemed to have triggered its predatory instincts. It was chasing him now. He could hear its footfalls – yeah, it had to be much bigger than a fox – following him.

It let out another cry, higher and longer, a real howl this time. Kyle's entire body went cold. What the hell was it? A dog? A *rabid* dog? A wolf? He didn't turn to look. That would only slow him down.

He took a sharp left, ducking around a tree, hoping to lose the . . . whatever was back there. It stayed with him. It was caught up in the hunt now. It let out another howl. Close. So close.

Kyle took another turn. Was he heading deeper into the woods? He wasn't sure – he'd lost track of the direction. And he didn't care. All he wanted was to get away. He could hear the creature breathing now, harsh eager pants.

Something sharp sliced across the back of his ankle, right between his sweats and the top of his sneaker. It took him a few seconds to register that he'd been bitten. Kyle pumped his legs and arms, reaching for every reserve of energy. It wasn't going to be enough.

The creature howled again. It was almost on him. Running wasn't going to work. Kyle whirled around, crouching into an attack position, his heart slamming against his ribs so hard he thought they would shatter.

There was nothing there. He scanned the darkening woods. Nothing. 'Where are you?' he shouted.

A howl answered him from so close that Kyle could feel hot breath on his face.

It was the last sound he'd ever hear.

Chapter One

'Hey, witchy baby.' Jess walked into Eve's room and dropped down on the bed next to her friend. She'd come over straight after her Monday afternoon cheer-leading practice.

'Remember, no witch stuff in front of my mom,' Eve reminded her best friend. Eve's mother didn't know Eve had discovered that she – and her mother – were descendants of the Deepdene Witch. Supposedly, at least according to Eve's dad, her mom had gotten teased relentlessly about it back in high school and she was sensitive about the whole thing.

Eve had a hard time believing her mother was or ever had been sensitive about anything. She was a heart surgeon, and she had the God complex that pretty much came with the job. But her father had said it would bother her mother if she knew Eve had discovered the truth about descending from a witch, although neither her mother nor her father believed that was the real deal. They thought villagers had called Eve's great-great-great-grandmother the Deepdene Witch because she'd been a little odd and had never remarried after her husband died young.

But Eve knew the truth. Her great-great-great gran had had the power to throw fire from her hands, a fire that could be used to battle demons. Unlike her mother, Eve had inherited the same ability.

'No worries. Your mom's all the way downstairs,' Jess answered.

'Good. I told her you, Luke and I were going to be up here studying. I left out the part about how we're going to be studying my fire-shooting woo-woo powers.' She couldn't believe it had only been a few months since those powers had started expressing themselves. She and Jess talked about them so casually.

'Leaving things out is pretty much the only way to handle parents,' Jess said. 'For example, I didn't mention that on Friday-night prowl we took the train to Brookhaven and tried to convince one of the guys at Tattoo Lou's that Jenna was old enough to get inked.'

Eve laughed. 'Yeah, I left that part out too. I said we

went to the movies. Which we did – after. How much fun was it though?'

'How much fun was what?' Luke asked, appearing in the doorway.

'Sorry. What happens on the prowl goes into the safe,' Jess told him.

'And the safe goes to the bottom of the ocean,' Eve added. 'Which, I gotta say, is where your jacket belongs,' she teased, smiling at him.

Luke ran his hand down the sleeve of his corduroy jacket. Yes, corduroy, with brown buttons that were definitely too big. 'What?' he asked.

'So many, many things,' Jess answered.

Yet somehow he still managed to look ultra-cute wearing the thing. The tan colour set off Luke's longish blond hair and those green eyes of his to perfection, even though the jacket looked like it should belong on some fifty-year-old college professor whose eighty-year-old mother still bought his clothes for him. Not Luke's usual style. Not that Luke put any thought into what his style was.

'Unlike you two, I have more important things to think about than clothes,' Luke said.

Eve shook her head. 'Look how he thinks that's something to brag about,' she told Jess. Although, since her town had been infested with demons a few months ago, Eve had started thinking about fashion a lot less. She, Eve Evergold, high-school freshman, had been the only one with the power to kill Malphas, the soul-stealing master demon.

At least Eve hoped that's what had happened. All she knew for sure was that Mal had disappeared along with his demon minions after she zapped him with every ounce of power she had in her body.

Luke took off the jacket and flung it over the back of Eve's desk chair. Then he opened his backpack and dumped a bunch of candles onto the bed between Eve and Jess. 'I thought these would be good for you to practise on. It seems like the thing you need most is control over your power. If you can figure out how to light a candle without melting it or blasting it apart, that'd be a good start.'

Jess picked up one of the candles and set it on the corner of Eve's desk. 'Try it, Evie.' She and Luke got settled on the bed to watch.

Eve nodded and stood up. For a wild moment she thought about asking if they wanted popcorn to eat during the show. Then she let everything non-essential fade from her mind. She shifted from foot to foot, shook out her hands and fingers, then went still.

She locked her gaze on the little votive candle and concentrated on feeling the power within her. She hadn't used it in a while, hadn't wanted to. She'd wanted to go back to regular life in her regular – celebrity-studded, millionaire-strewn – little town.

But off and on she'd smelled wood-smoke. The smell she associated with the demon Malphas and his minions. It was fall. Wood-smoke wasn't an out-of-the-ordinary scent, but Eve needed to be ready in case the smell wasn't coming from fireplaces or bonfires. That was the whole point of today's 'study' session.

She pulled in a long, slow breath and released it just as slowly. She was fully charged. She could feel the power there, waiting for her, a bright, hot reservoir. Eve narrowed her focus down to the candle's wick. She needed to give it a flick of power, just a quick touch.

Her fingertips began to vibrate as she readied herself. She heard her hair start to crackle with electricity. The sensations jerked her back to that final moment with Malphas, who'd stood in front of her looking like the boy she'd been crushing on, with his chocolate-brown eyes, his crooked smile.

Revulsion cut through Eve and her power burst from her fingers in long bolts of fire-edged lightning.

The candle exploded. A tiny piece of wax struck Eve on the cheek. The velocity made it as hard as a pebble. She rubbed the sore spot with her thumb. 'Maybe we should have borrowed some safety equipment from the bio lab. Some goggles at least.' She looked over at her friends. 'You OK?' They both nodded.

Luke flicked a tiny piece of wax off the knee of his jeans. 'So what happened with the . . .' He opened his hands, making one of those explosion noises that boys seemed to learn before they acquired language.

'I – I thought about Mal,' Eve admitted. 'And I just lost it.'

'My mom just brought some goggles for Ringo – well, sunglass goggles,' Jess said, picking a piece of wax out of one of her short braids. 'They're called Doggles. She read that UV light is as bad for dogs' eyes as it is for humans'. Next time I'll bring them. They're actually kind of cute.' Jess was the best at coming up with a little distracting chatter when it was needed most. Eve definitely needed a moment to recover.

'Would it be OK if I puke in your wastebasket?' Luke asked Eve. 'I'm not sure I can make it to the bathroom.'

'You're going to criticize Ringo the poodle's fashion

choices when you came in wearing that?' Eve nodded towards the jacket on the back of the chair.

'Yes. Yes, I am,' Luke answered. 'Dogs shouldn't have fashion choices. They should have a leash, a collar, a couple of tags. That's it.'

Eve grabbed another candle and set it in position at the edge of her desk. She was doing this. She pictured that reservoir of liquid light inside her. She pictured herself dipping a bottle in and filling it. Her arms began to feel fizzy inside, as if warm champagne were flowing down them, the bubbles gently popping. *That's right. Nice and easy*, she coached herself. She raised her arms, aiming her hands at the candle, keeping her eyes on the wick.

The fizzy feeling intensified, the bubbles popping fast. *Now!* Her fingers turned to sparklers, but the dashes of light didn't come close to reaching the candle, even though it was only about two metres away.

'What were you thinking about that time?' Jess asked.

'Tinky Winky,' Eve answered. She and Jess had had a serious *Teletubbies* obsession for a few months during kindergarten. They'd only answer people when they were addressed by the Tubby names they'd come up with for themselves. 'Actually I wasn't really thinking about anything except the power. I was visualizing it, trying to keep it in check.'

'Emotion has a big part in the strength of your power,' Luke reminded her. He would know. The very first time her power had started expressing itself, Luke had been teasing her and out came the sparks.

They'd barely known each other. And what Eve *had* known she hadn't really liked. But Luke had stepped up. He'd been by her side – along with Jess – through almost every moment of the demon crisis.

'Shall we taunt you?' Jess sounded a little too eager. 'Or you could just think about Luke's jacket.'

'Are we still on that?' he protested.

'For a few more days at least,' Eve told him, shooting him a wink. She walked over to the desk and straightened the candle's wick. *Because, yeah, that was definitely the problem: crooked wick*, she thought as she backed up into her zapping position.

Almost half an hour later she was putting her twelfth candle into position. 'What's the score?' she asked Luke.

'Seven explosions, four meltings, the one where you knocked the candle off the table and four fizzles.'

'Fizzies,' Jess corrected. 'We decided to call them fizzies.'

'They're all going to be fizzies, or whatever we're calling them, pretty soon,' Eve said. 'I'm losing juice.' She could only zap for so long without her power getting too low to even send sparks from her fingers. The bigger the zap, the more power got used up. 'Come on, lucky number twelve,' she called, flexing her fingers a few times.

'I didn't know twelve was lucky,' Luke said to Jess.

'Come on. Twelve, like a dozen. Good things come in dozens,' Eve explained.

'Lords a-leaping,' Jess offered.

'It's drummers drumming,' Luke corrected. 'I'm a minister's kid. I know every hymn and carol there is.'

'Drummers drumming.' Jess smiled. 'I like. Drummers are sexy.'

'I was thinking more like cookies or, yum, donuts, but OK,' Eve said. She gave her fingers one last flex. 'Here goes.'

She felt the fizzing move from her chest across her shoulders. *Harder*, she urged herself as the tickling sensation moved down her arms. In response, the current moved faster, and the bubbles felt as if they were coming to a boil. Bigger and with more of a *ping* when they popped. *This could be it!* she thought as she let the power surge out of her fingers.

A beautiful bolt of orange-tinged lightning zig-zagged across the room. When the tip touched the wick, the candle lit. The small yellow flame was a beautiful, beautiful sight.

'Woo-hoo!' Jess cried.

'Woo-hoo!' Eve echoed, exhilaration filling her . . . until the candle began to smoulder as the wick sank down into the quickly melting wax.

Eve began to drop her arms But she jerked them back up as a high-pitched shriek cut through the room. Her heart slammed against her ribs. Her power slammed through her body. Too late, she realized that the sound was only the smoke detector. She couldn't stop her power from jumping free with a crackling whoosh. A second later flames were consuming Luke's jacket.

'What's going on?' Eve's mother called from downstairs.

'Smoke detector! Candle!' Eve shouted back. 'We got it.'

Jess started whacking at the jacket with one of Eve's pillows while Luke dumped his Coke over it. Eve grabbed another pillow and waved it under the smoke detector. The wreck that was her room – burned jacket, plus tortured candles, plus bits of wax everywhere – was not something she wanted to have to explain to her mom.

She waved the pillow harder. The jacket fire was out, but the burned corduroy – yes, corduroy – was still producing a lot of smoke. She dropped the pillow, dashed over to the windows and threw them all open. The alarm was still squealing.

She grabbed her desk chair, swept the jacket off it, then dragged the chair across the room, climbed onto it and ripped the batteries out of the alarm. It finally shut up. 'See, Mom. It was nothing!' she yelled as she stepped back down. 'We'd better clean this place,' she told Jess and Luke. 'My power is getting really low anyway. That last blast took a lot.'

'But for a second you got it,' Jess said. 'You lit the candle perfectly.'

'Yeah, I did.' *After more than a dozen tries*, she silently added. She needed a lot more practice if she was going to be able to control her power. She caught a whiff of smoke. Not from the candles. Wood-smoke. Drifting in through the open windows.

Was something out there? Something evil? Something like Mal?

I have to keep practising. Practising, practising, practising, Eve thought. *I have to be ready . . . for anything.*

'You did this on purpose. Don't even try to deny it,' Luke accused, and Jess began to giggle.

Eve turned and saw him staring at the soggy, smouldering ruins of his jacket. 'I didn't. I swear. In a war there will be casualties.' She moved up next to him and wrapped an arm around his shoulders. *Some nice muscles there*, she couldn't help noticing.

For a few seconds they stared in silence at what remained of the jacket. 'And, Luke, you gotta know,' Eve added, 'it was truly hideous.'

Chapter Two

'Eve, Eve, OMG, you're not going to believe this!' Jess cried as she raced down the hallway towards her best friend on Tuesday morning at school.

'What? We've only been apart for twenty minutes – and nothing exciting ever happens in homeroom,' Eve replied. She opened her locker and quickly checked her lipstick in the mirror on the inside of the door.

'I wasn't in homeroom. Vic and I got permission to use the office Xerox machine to cop—' Jess stopped mid-sentence. 'Doesn't matter what we were copying. Just cheerleading stuff. What matters is that the chief of police was in the principal's office, and he was telling her that Kyle Rakoff's dead!' she finished in a rush.

Eve shivered as power whispered through her body, sizzling. She wrapped her arms around herself as if that would help her control it. She knew from past experience that intense emotion made it unstable.

'Kyle? But he's my lab partner. I saw him just yesterday,' Eve protested. As if having seen him yesterday meant that he couldn't possibly be dead. 'What happened?'

'They aren't sure. Chief Grotte just said that they found his body in the woods. It wasn't easy to identify him.' Jess pressed her hand against her throat. 'He was . . . He was all torn up. His face and everything. Just torn to pieces. They didn't know who it was right away.'

A locker slammed behind Eve, even though no one was close enough to touch it. *I did that*, Eve realized. Her power was rising out of her control. She had to get a grip before she started accidentally setting things on fire, because that was never pretty. She started her trying-to-calm-down slow breathing.

'You all good?' Jess asked. 'You're not going to kapow, are you?' Most of the time Jess could tell what was going on with Eve just by looking at her. Same way Eve could almost tell what Jess was thinking by the expression on Jess's face. What BFFs couldn't?

Eve shook her head, making her dark ringlets bounce. 'No, I'm OK.' She took another deep breath, trying to let go of the image of Kyle's body ripped and ravaged. 'What else did you hear?'

'Not much. The receptionist made me and Vic leave when she realized we were listening. But on our way out I heard the chief say that Kyle had been drained of blood.' Jess looked as if some of her blood had been drained too. Her face was pale, pale, pale.

'There's a cop car out front. I saw from the first-floor windows when I was coming down here,' Dave Perry called out from the row of lockers across the hall. 'What's the deal?'

'You guys, the police are here,' Megan Christie, Jess's next-door neighbour, exclaimed as she hurried out of the bathroom. One of her eyelids had more shadow than the other. 'Jenna just texted me.' She glanced at her cellphone. 'She says Kyle got murdered.'

'Murdered?' Dave burst out.

The bell rang. They all ignored it. Even the teachers standing in their classroom doorways didn't start ordering kids in the way they usually would.

'Not murdered. At least, not definitely,' Jess corrected them. 'I was in the office. Chief Grotte told Principal Allison that they found Kyle's body in the woods.'

'That's not what I heard. Jenna told me that Victoria said—' Megan began.

'I was with Vic,' Jess interrupted, smoothing her

blonde hair away from her face. 'I heard the same thing she did, and they didn't say it was murder.'

Shanna Poplin rounded the corner with the new girl, Briony, at her heels. 'Did you guys hear about Kyle?' Shanna asked. 'Vic just texted me to say—'

Eve's own iPhone buzzed, rattling against the metal shelf of her locker. That's where it lived during classes, since cellphones weren't allowed. She grabbed it and checked the screen. 'She's texting me now. I don't know why she didn't just do a mass one.' Eve shrugged. 'Would have been easier.'

'I've got to call my mom. She's going to be freaking if it's on the news,' Jess said. She plucked Eve's cell from her hand, but it rang before she had a chance to use it. 'Eve's phone,' Jess answered it. 'She's right next to me, Mr Evergold. She's fine. We're all fine. Except Kyle.' Her voice broke on his name, and a sheen of tears appeared in her bright blue eyes. She gave the phone back to Eve.

'I'm really, really fine, Dad. The police chief is here,' Eve told her father.

'Are they sending everybody home?' her dad asked, his tone worried. 'Do you want me to come get you?'

'They haven't said anything about us going home,' Eve said. Jess plucked at her sleeve, her eyebrows raised. Eve knew exactly what she wanted. 'Dad, will you call Jess's mom?' she asked. 'If you're worried, the other parents probably are too.'

'Well, when you hear about a classmate of your daughter found dead . . .' Her dad's voice trailed off for a moment. 'You're right,' he said. 'All the parents must be panicking. Not everyone is as level-headed as me.' He was going for a joking tone, but Eve could tell he was freaked.

'Sad but true,' Eve said, smiling a little.

'I'll talk to Jess's mother first. Your mom's in the O.R. so I'll wait to speak to her. You call me if you need anything.'

'I will. Thanks, Daddy.' Eve hung up. 'He's calling your mom first. He's going to call my mom when she's out of surgery. She won't have heard about what happened yet,' Eve told Jess. 'She only listens to Johnny Cash when she's operating.'

Why was she telling Jess that? Jess already knew about her mom's Johnny Cash fetish. *Talking keeps me from thinking,* Eve realized. And the last thing she wanted to do was to think about Kyle lying in the woods, the earth soaked with his blood.

'Listen to this, you guys,' Shanna said, eyes on her BlackBerry. '*The Times* already has something up.

Probably because Kyle's grandfather is a senator. It says that Kyle didn't come home last night.'

'They called me,' Dave said. He blinked rapidly, distraught. 'His parents were looking for him. I said I saw him leave practice and I was pretty sure he was heading home, then to Ola's. That's what he told me. I went to Ola's later, didn't see him around. I figured – I just thought – you know Kyle. I thought . . .' Dave fell silent, staring into space.

'Kyle's Kyle,' Jess said gently. Except he wasn't. Not any more.

Dave nodded. 'But I should have—'

'You shouldn't have anything,' Eve interrupted. 'How could you know? Kyle didn't always stick to his plans.'

'He followed the fun,' Dave agreed. He turned away from the group, pretending he urgently needed something in his locker. Eve thought he might be crying.

Shanna was, but it didn't stop her giving them more information from the article. 'The police say it was a wild-animal attack, but the medical examiner hasn't yet determined what kind of animal. The animal would have to be really . . .' Her words trailed off.

'Really what?' Jess asked. Her voice sounded way

too loud. Eve realized it was because the hallway had gone silent. Not just their group. Everyone had stopped talking almost at once.

It took Eve only a second to figure out why. Helena was coming down the hall. She had a little smile on her face and her long blonde hair looked freshly brushed. Her lipstick looked fresh too. *Oh, God. She hasn't heard*, Eve thought. *We're going to have to tell her.*

Jess took a few steps towards Helena. Helena wasn't part of their super-tight group of friends, but she and Jess were on the cheerleading squad together. Or at least they had been until Helena got dropped because of her grades.

'Helena . . .' Jess swallowed hard. 'Something's happened. Something bad. Kyle—'

'I know,' Helena interrupted. 'They found his body in the woods. I was just in the principal's office. Ms Allison and the police chief told me.' It sounded like she was passing on a regular bit of Deepdene High gossip. Almost matter-of-fact.

She blinked a few times. 'They just told me,' she repeated, her voice beginning to quaver. 'He's dead. Kyle's dead.' She pressed both hands over her mouth as if she could push the horrible words back in.

Delayed reaction, Eve realized. *It only just hit her.*

'Helena!' Ms Allison's high heels clicked on the floor as she hurried over. 'Helena, I meant for you to stay in the office. I've called your father. He's coming to pick you up.'

'Kyle.' That's all she managed to say before she broke into loud wrenching sobs. Not the pretty crying girls do in movies. The horrible out-of-control crying where your face gets all blotchy and your nose runs and you feel like you'll never, ever be able to stop.

Ms Allison wrapped her arm around Helena's shoulders and walked her back down the hall towards the office. There was absolute silence – except for Helena's ragged crying – until they had rounded the corner.

Dave cursed under his breath.

'Poor Helena. She showed up at school thinking it was another regular day, then – bam!' Shanna said.

'I can't even imagine how she must feel,' Jess added. 'She has to be devastated. And so soon after her mom . . .'

'I can't believe I actually forgot about that,' Eve admitted as they started for the main exit. Helena's mother had died the previous month, right after the demon Malphas had begun taking the souls of people in Deepdene.

He hadn't had anything to do with Mrs Groshart's death. She'd had a heart attack. Eve had been so caught up trying to figure out what her new powers were and how they could be used to stop the demon that she'd hardly registered the passing of Helena's mother.

'Um, can I ask something?' Briony said.

'Sure,' Eve answered. Briony's eyes had widened as she'd watched everyone talking and crying.

'Are there really wild animals around here?' Briony asked. She'd only been at their school for a week. She didn't know anything about Deepdene yet.

'Not really,' Eve assured her. 'I mean, there are foxes. Other than that, there are just some squirrels and raccoons, and the brown bunnies in the scrub brush down near the beach. And deer, but obviously they're not dangerous.'

'Once in a while summer people abandon their dogs when they go back to New York City for the winter,' Jess said. 'It's so horrible. They treat them like toys. The poor dogs are used to someone feeding them and taking care of them, then nothing. They can go kind of wild.'

'What an introduction to Deepdene,' Megan said. 'Our sweet little town, population two thousand seven hundred and something, where nothing ever happens.'

'Yeah,' Briony agreed sadly.

This isn't the worst our little town has to offer, Eve thought. But she wasn't about to tell the new girl about the demonic happenings in this village in the Hamptons. Most people thought of the area as a swanky vacation spot three hours east of Manhattan, with beautiful beaches, lovely woods and hills and fabulous mansions and famous residents. Nobody expected demon attacks and wild animals in Deepdene.

A chilling thought hit Eve. There really weren't the kind of wild animals in the Hamptons that could have killed Kyle. Were they dealing with something else here? Something unearthly?

Luke jogged up to the cluster of people. 'Hey, guys. I just heard that Principal Allison is going to send everybody home,' he announced.

Eve felt herself relax the second she heard his voice. She hadn't even realized she'd been looking for him until he arrived. Luke was a guy you wanted around when things got bad – smart, loyal, brave. And things were bad now.

'Deepdene *is* usually a quiet town, Briony. Really,' Shanna assured her.

Everyone still believed that – except for Eve, Jess and Luke. They'd faced down the demons together. Jess wrapped her arms around Eve and gave her a hard hug. Eve knew she was thinking about the demons too. They did that a lot, thinking the same thing at the same time, and called it being 'telefriendic'. The way Luke was looking at them both right now, his green eyes steady and serious, gave Eve the feeling he was having a telefriendic moment of his own.

'So we're just supposed to leave?' Briony asked.

'There'll be an official announcement in a minute,' Luke told her. 'I'm just the early warning system.'

'It feels weird to go home after something like this,' Briony said.

'No one's going home,' Luke answered. 'Everyone will spend the day of mourning shopping and eating ice cream at Ola's. If they aren't having coffee at Java Nation.' He turned and started off down the hallway. 'More people to inform,' he added over his shoulder.

Briony stared after him, mouth agape.

'Luke has a strange sense of humour sometimes,'

Eve said, right before Ms Allison's voice came over the loudspeakers, notifying the students and faculty that school would be closed for the day out of respect for Kyle's death.

'So people aren't really going to eat ice cream and stuff?' Briony asked as the group began to disperse.

'Actually they probably will,' Jess admitted. 'But not in a bad way. Not like, "Yee-haw, we have a day off." More like people will want to be together because it's so horrible, and Main Street is where people go to get together.'

Briony nodded slowly. 'OK. Well . . . maybe I'll see you over there later.' She wandered away.

'I'm definitely heading over to Ola's after I go home to show my mom I'm alive.' Shanna clapped her hand over her mouth. 'Oh no! That sounded hideous.'

Eve waved her comment off. 'We knew what you meant. Don't worry.'

'Thanks. I guess I'll stop by my locker first.' Shanna looked a little dazed as she headed off.

'Let's get out of here too,' Jess suggested. 'I could use some air.'

Eve put her books in her locker and closed it gently. No homework that night.

She and Jess walked down the hall towards Jess's

locker. 'I wonder if Luke blew it with Briony with his *unusual* sense of humour,' Jess said.

'You think he's interested in her?' Eve asked.

'She's new. And she's cute. And our Luke is a player. So . . . yes,' Jess said. She let out a groan. 'I can't believe I'm even talking about that. How can I be thinking about anything but Kyle?'

'Thinking about Kyle is too awful. My mind keeps jerking away from it. I think about him for one or two seconds, and I start seeing all that blood – there had to be so much – and then . . . Then it's like my brain hits the circuit-breaker.' Eve lowered her voice. There were still lots of people milling around. 'At least it's helping me keep my powers under control. When you first told me—'

'I saw that locker slam,' Jess said. 'But don't worry, no one else noticed. Too much else going on.' She opened her own locker and stowed her history book and binder. 'So Briony and Luke? Since we're trying not to think about Kyle too much.'

Eve didn't really want to think about Briony and Luke either. Not that Luke was anything but a friend to her. They definitely weren't boyfriend-girlfriend; not like . . .

'Do you think Helena knew . . .?' Eve waited until

she and Jess had stepped outside to finish the question. 'Do you think she knew that Kyle wasn't exactly devoted? I don't know if it's better or worse if she did.'

'She never said anything to me,' Jess answered. 'But it's not like Kyle was exactly subtle.'

'Yeah. He asked me out for coffee about a million times, and he didn't seem to care who heard it. I started to wonder if he thought I didn't realize he was going out with Helena.'

'But that's crazy. Everybody knows everything at our school. There just aren't enough of us to hide anything,' Jess said. 'So Helena either knew, or she kind of knew but decided to pretend she didn't know. You know?'

Eve stopped abruptly.

'What?' Jess asked.

'Kyle asked me out yesterday during bio lab. That was the last time I talked to him.' Eve grabbed her friend's arm. 'And I was so horrible. I really snapped at him. I just thought it was so disrespectful of him when he was supposed to be Helena's boyfriend.' Tears stung her eyes. 'I wish that hadn't been our last conversation. He was kind of a jerk with all the flirting. But he was also funny and, basically, in other ways, just a good guy.'

'I know. I can't believe he's really gone,' Jess said. They started walking again, heading towards Main Street without discussing it. Two and a half blocks of the street were crammed with shops and restaurants, and it really was the only place in town to go.

'Now I can't stop thinking about what I said,' Eve murmured. 'It's like I have our whole talk on a loop.'

'Let it go,' Jess told her. 'You've known Kyle for ever. We all have. You've had hundreds and hundreds of conversations with him between first grade and . . . and yesterday. The last one isn't the most important one.'

Eve let out a sigh that felt as though it started deep in her belly. 'I thought we'd gotten through the horribleness, you know?' she told Jess. 'I thought after I defeated Malphas, after he was gone . . . I guess I thought that the rest of the year would be calm. That everything would go back to normal.'

'Yeah. Me too.'

Eve felt as if inky darkness had flooded her soul, weighing it down. 'But now I'm starting to wonder if it's possible for Deepdene to ever be normal again.'

Chapter Three

Luke stepped through the bright yellow front door of Big Ola's and took a look around. Yep, the place was packed, just as he'd expected. Not that that was bad. People needed to be together when they were grieving or afraid. He'd seen that over and over at the rectory and at the many funerals his father had presided over as a minister, and the wakes and receptions they'd gone to together.

'Thompson! Over here.' James Frankel waved and pointed to the empty chair next to him. A bunch of kids from school had pushed three of the little café tables together. Luke walked over and joined them, at the same time glancing around for Eve – Eve and Jess. He didn't see them, which was weird. He'd been almost positive that they would be here. They were pretty much the centre of Deepdene High's most popular group.

'Can someone walk me home later?' Victoria Matthews asked, putting down her cell. 'My mother is sure that in the two blocks between here and there I'll be mauled, without someone to protect me.'

Her tone was exasperated, but Luke caught a whiff of underlying fear. And Vic seemed a little relieved when Alexander Neemy immediately volunteered before Luke even had the chance to open his mouth.

Victoria would be more than a little scared if she knew what had been happening in town a few weeks ago, Luke thought. Several of her good friends had had their souls sucked out by the demon Malphas. If Eve didn't have the powers passed down by the Deepdene Witch, the only place Vic would be able to see those friends was in a mental hospital.

Luke did another check for Eve. She might be the protector of the town, but he kind of felt like he was the protector of *her*.

'I guess my parents aren't the only ones who've jumped to Code Red,' Dave said. He downed a giant spoonful of his mudslide sundae.

'I think your parents were right to make you cancel your camping trip,' Vic told him. 'Walking two blocks on the sidewalk in the middle of the day is one thing.

Camping in the woods overnight – that's something else. Something crazy stupid else.'

'There's nothing out there I can't handle,' Dave insisted.

'Yeah, don't forget Dave has his trusty potato gun,' James said. Everyone laughed for about two seconds, then suddenly fell silent, as if they'd all remembered at the same moment that Kyle was dead.

'Potato gun?' Luke asked. He'd only moved to Deepdene a few months ago, while almost everyone else had lived here their whole lives. There was still a lot of inside stuff he didn't get.

'Dave really wanted a BB gun for his eighth birthday. That's all he talked about for six months beforehand,' Jenna Barton explained.

'And then he got one of those guns that shoots potato pellets instead,' Luke guessed.

Jenna shook her head. 'No, he got the BB. Shot himself in the foot less than a half an hour after he unwrapped it.'

'It could have happened to anyone!' Dave protested.

'So of course the BB got taken away,' Jenna went on, 'and he got the tater gun as a replacement. No replacement for that bit of toe though.'

Everyone laughed again. Softly. Funeral-reception laughter.

'I heard some people are planning to buy *real* guns – at least until the animal that . . . that got Kyle is caught,' Vic commented. Luke noticed she'd had trouble coming up with a more accurate word, like 'killed' or 'mauled'.

Phoebe, one of the regular Ola's waitresses, stopped by. She had to be almost thirty years old, but she looked just as spooked and upset as the kids from school. Luke ordered a vanilla shake with a shot of espresso. As she stepped away he heard the bells on the front door ring out. He immediately looked over, and a smile spread across his face. Eve and Jess.

He got up and hurried over to them. 'Gossip exchange,' Jess commanded, instead of saying hello.

'Victoria can't walk home without an escort, Dave can't go camping this weekend and on my way here I heard that Mr Groshart has Helena locked in her room on suicide watch,' Luke answered obediently.

'We saw Helena's father while we were on our way here. He'd just gotten a couple of frappuccinos from Java Nation to take home for him and Helena,' Eve said. 'He said Helena's upset, and that she'll probably take some days off school until she's had time to adjust. But he was out buying coffees for them, and didn't seem worried that she was alone, so I think the suicide watch thing definitely falls into the "false rumour" column.'

Luke nodded. 'Oh, I forgot: there may be a spike in gun buying.' Luke knew that when Jess asked for gossip, she wanted it all.

'You know, if I wasn't afraid of guns, I might get one,' Jess said.

'A gun would ruin the line of every outfit you wore,' Eve teased gently.

'Also, and admittedly much less important than the outfit thing, it would be illegal. You're still a minor,' Luke pointed out. He pushed his blond hair out of his face. He liked it long, but it had been a while since his last haircut and it was almost to the point where there would be vision impairment.

'But I need some protection against the mountain lion. Maybe a knife in a little sheath strapped to my thigh?' Jess said. 'With that plaid Catholic-schoolgirl-esque miniskirt of mine, it could be hot.'

Eve nodded. 'In a badass anime-heroine way.'

'Exactly,' Jess agreed.

'Back up. Mountain lion?' Luke asked.

'On our way over we heard it was a mountain

lion that killed Kyle,' Eve said, exasperated. Luke noticed that Eve hadn't had any trouble saying the word 'killed'. It made him a little sad. When he'd first met her, she would've been more skittish, like Vic. But Eve had changed. He had too, actually. Experiencing evil at such close range did that.

'I've been telling Jess that there aren't any mountain lions on Long Island,' Eve continued. 'Or anywhere within a thousand miles.'

'And I've been telling Eve that global weather changes have caused weird animal migration patterns,' Jess said. Luke raised his eyebrows. He was surprised to hear such a scientific theory coming from Jess. 'I'm not stupid,' she informed him, noting his reaction. 'And besides, my brother likes to watch the Discovery Channel.'

'Much as I'd like to see you with a dagger strapped to your thigh – you too, Eve,' he added with a wink, 'I'm sure the police and animal control will be able to handle this solo.'

'So you don't think this is anything abnormal?' Eve asked. 'I mean, of course it's abnormal, but is it *extreme* abnormal?'

'I don't think we have to go there,' Luke answered.

'Please let's not go there,' Jess added.

'Horrible things happen sometimes,' Luke went on. 'It's life. Normal, hugely sucky, life.' He looped one arm around Jess's shoulders and one around Eve's waist. 'How about you two smokin' babes let me buy you an ice cream?'

'Let's hope that's not your A game, player,' Eve joked.

'Is that a "yes"?' Luke asked.

Eve gave a queenly nod. 'Yes, you may buy us ice cream. You may also procure chairs for us.'

Luke looked around the crowded room, spotted a couple of free chairs and carried them over to his table. 'My ladies,' he said to Eve and Jess.

'We have the new boy well trained, don't we?' Jess asked as they all sat down with their friends.

'You two can train me if you want to,' Dave said. 'I'm open to most types of discipline.'

'How much longer am I going to be the new boy?' Luke asked.

'Until we have another one,' Vic told him. 'You could still be the new boy a year from now.'

Phoebe put Luke's glass down, the frosty silver shaker next to it. 'I'll be back for your orders in a few, girls,' she told Eve and Jess. 'The place is, well – look around.' Luke didn't think he'd ever seen the café so crowded, even in the summer, with all the tourists.

'OK, I started looking for more info about animals around here. This site says that foxes and big birds – the hawk kind, not the yellow googly-eyed kind with a person inside – are the only real predators in the Hamptons.' Jess fiddled with her BlackBerry. 'I can take a fox or a bird barehanded, although it might mess up my manicure.'

Another one of those silences fell across the table. Eve quickly broke it. She pressed one hand over her heart. 'You're not suggesting Big Bird has a person inside, are you?'

Nice save, Luke thought as their friends broke into relieved laughter. The group clearly wanted a break from thinking about wild animals. And what a wild animal had done to Kyle.

'I used to be afraid of Big Bird,' James admitted. 'He was just so–'

'Big?' Vic offered.

'Yellow,' James said.

'What does that even mean?' Eve asked. 'Were you afraid of other yellow things?'

'Rubber duckies? Bananas?' Jess suggested.

'Forget it, OK? Just forget it. Never should have brought it up,' James told them, clearly realizing that the group could spend the next half-hour at least analysing his yellow phobia. 'Luke, you saw Kyle after school yesterday, right?'

'At football practice, yeah,' Luke answered. He'd been asked the same question about five times already.

'Did he seem weird or anything?' James asked.

Luke shook his head. 'Same as always. Same killer tackle, same bad jokes, same . . .'

Jess's phone rang. She rolled her eyes as she checked to see who it was. 'Mom,' she mouthed to Eve, then answered. 'I have safely made it from the sidewalk in front of Jildor's to inside Ola's,' Luke heard her say. 'OK . . . OK . . . OK,' Jess continued, then hung up.

She sighed. 'I think I'm going to go home. My mother has been calling, I swear, every five minutes. No exaggeration.'

Eve stood up. 'I'll go with you.'

'Thanks, Evie. We have a ton of ice cream at home. Unless Peter has piggied it all.' Peter was Jess's younger brother.

'See you guys tomorrow,' Eve told everyone. Jess gave a wave. Luke walked them over to the door. 'Want me to come with?'

'We're fine. Stay and drink your milkshake,' Eve answered.

The door opened and Briony came in. 'You're already leaving?' she asked them.

'We are, but Luke's not,' Jess answered. She gave Luke a smirk. 'That's his table over there.' She pointed to the table they'd just left. 'Grab one of the empty seats before someone else does.'

'Thanks.' Briony headed that way.

Luke took a step after her, then turned back. 'You're sure you don't want me to come with you?'

'Go!' Eve insisted. 'Briony's the new girl. You're contractually obligated to flirt with her or we'll have to take your player licence away.'

Luke pointed at Jess and Eve and made texting motions with his thumbs. 'Let me know when you get there, OK?'

Eve smiled at him. 'Yes, Daddy.' She opened the door and led the way out. Luke watched for a moment as the two girls started down the sidewalk. Eve was gesturing wildly as she talked. He realized she'd been even more animated than usual since she came into Ola's. *Trying to push the badness away*, he thought.

He returned to his seat. 'Glad you came,' he told Briony. 'I thought maybe I'd scared you off.'

'Eve told me that you had a strange sense of humour, and everyone kind of explained that this wasn't a completely insensitive thing to do,' Briony answered.

'I'll have to thank Eve for interpreting,' Luke joked. 'I hope I won't need her to explain me too often.' Although if anybody could do it, Eve could. She was starting to know him better than anyone else. Which wasn't necessarily a good thing. He hoped she didn't go around passing out stats on how many girls he'd gone out with since he'd arrived in Deepdene. She seemed to have them memorized and think he was some kind of hound, even though Luke would describe himself as just your basic, friendly guy.

A little friendlier to cute girls, he could almost hear Eve add. Well, she should know, being a cute girl herself.

Luke took a gulp of his milkshake – forgetting, the way he always did, about brain freeze. When the cold pain receded from behind his eyes, he realized that a new person had taken a seat at the table behind theirs. He couldn't see the guy that well as Briony was blocking the view.

Luke slid his chair a little to the right until he caught a glimpse of the guy's profile. He was old, maybe in his thirties, and his face was unfamiliar. He had on a beat-up, dirty trench coat and battered cowboy boots. He wasn't from Deepdene. Which, Luke had lived here long enough to know, was weird. Once the summer ended, it was pretty much regulars at Ola's and everyplace else in Deepdene, especially on a weekday.

'Hey, Luke, did Jess or Eve say anything about Helena?' Jenna asked, interrupting his thoughts. 'Is she really suicidal?'

'They saw her dad getting coffee like everything was normal. They don't think she's in any danger.' Luke caught a jerk of motion out of the corner of his eye. The guy behind Briony was taking notes, typing furiously into his laptop. Luke shook his head. He should have realized right away that stranger after tragedy equalled reporter.

He stood up. 'That's off the record, by the way,' he said more loudly.

'I'm with the *New York Post*,' the guy announced, acting like it was nothing to have been caught eavesdropping. 'I'm here to cover the tragic death of Kyle Rakoff. Did any of you know him?'

'I've known him since nursery school,' Jenna answered eagerly. 'He was the greatest, greatest guy.'

Her voice quavered a little. Luke believed she was sad about Kyle. He also believed Jenna wasn't minding the reporter's attention. At all.

'He was one of my best friends,' Dave added. 'Like a brother.'

Suddenly the milkshake didn't taste so good. The reporter trolling for any little detail about Kyle felt wrong. Luke dropped some money on the table. 'I'm heading off.'

He got some 'bye's and 'see you's as he walked out. From the sidewalk he could see the tips of the trees in the woods where Kyle had died. He hoped he'd been right when he told Eve that Kyle's death was part of the sucky side of normal life, and not . . . something else.

If it is, Eve won't have to deal with it alone, he promised himself. Yes, sometimes Eve Evergold was annoying. She could be a little too sensitive, and she spent a ridiculous amount of money on purses.

But she was a force for good in the world, and it was his responsibility to back her up. And he was positive that he'd feel the same way even if she wasn't extraordinarily adorable.

*

'I think every teacher Kyle ever had is here, and everybody from our class,' Eve said softly as she glanced around the church. All the pews were packed with people for his funeral. It was hard to believe it had already been three days since they heard about Kyle's death.

'Not just our class, the whole school,' Jess commented, nodding towards Megan, who was in the back with her boyfriend of the week. Megan was a sophomore, while Eve and Jess were freshmen. 'Plus everyone's parents.' Eve's and Jess's parents were sitting together a few rows behind them.

'Mr Enslow from the hardware store is here,' Eve noted. 'He doesn't have any kids at high school now. Did he even really know Kyle?'

'He was Kyle's Little League coach. Peter was on that team too,' Jess replied. 'My parents always made me go watch the games with them.' Deepdene was so small that almost every person in the town was connected, with at most one degree of separation.

But there were a bunch of people in the church Eve didn't recognize at all. Some of them, the ones up in the front, were probably Kyle's out-of-town relatives. But the ones all the way in the back had to be reporters. In the four days since the police had found Kyle's body the papers had been full of stories about his death and speculation regarding what exactly had killed him. There hadn't been any progress in tracking down the animal – whatever it was.

Eve wished the reporters had stayed outside the church. This time should be for people who cared about Kyle. It didn't feel right to have strangers here, folks who'd never even met him or his family.

Luke stepped up to the pulpit, adjusted the microphone and set out a pitcher of water and a glass. His expression was solemn as he took a seat in one of the pews. Was it wrong to notice how good he looked in his dark blue suit – none of it corduroy – with his long blond hair swept back off his face? Eve felt it was a little wrong, but she couldn't help noticing what she noticed.

Jess leaned closer. 'Helena just came in.'

Eve tilted her head just far enough to watch Helena walking down the centre aisle. Her black cowl-neck tunic dress set off long blonde hair perfectly, although her face was drawn and pale. Her eyes were bright and glittery, as if she had a fever.

Jess nodded with approval. 'Good for Helena,' she whispered in Eve's ear. 'She's clearly wrecked, but has pulled herself together. She's going to be OK.'

Eve nodded in agreement. She let her gaze wander to the gargoyles that stared down from the ceiling, dozens and dozens of them. As often as she'd looked at them, she still saw new things every time. Today she noticed that a tiny woman stood on the protruding tongue of a stone figure with a horrific grimace.

As terrifying and ugly as some of the gargoyles were, Eve loved them all. They had saved her life. The gargoyles protected the church from demons. She, along with Jess and Luke, had found safety here when they needed it most.

Eve returned her attention to the front of the church as Ms Hahn began to play 'Calling All Angels' on the organ. When she finished Luke's father, Reverend Thompson, took his place at the pulpit.

'Welcome,' he said gravely. 'We are gathered here today to celebrate the life and mourn the death of Kyle Rakoff.' Eve reached out and took Jess's hand. This was only the second funeral she'd been to. The first was for her great-aunt, who had died at the age of eighty-seven. That had been sad, but right somehow. No, right wasn't the word she wanted. Appropriate? Expected?

All the relatives had kept saying, 'She lived a good life.' That was the thing. Kyle hadn't. He should have had so many more years of life to live. It felt so hugely unfair that he didn't. That was the difference. Her great-aunt's death had been sad, but not tragic, because even though it was a complete cliché, she had lived for a long time and gotten to do all the things she wanted to, and that meant something.

Eve realized she'd been so caught up in her own thoughts that she hadn't been following what Reverend Thompson was saying. She refocused. 'Kyle will be missed by all of us. But his memory will live in our hearts as long as we ourselves live.' Then he asked if anyone wanted to share a memory about Kyle.

Mrs Rakoff stood up. She opened her lips to speak, but then her face contorted and she started to cry. She held out her hands helplessly.

'Take your time,' Reverend Thompson said, but Kyle's mom shook her head. Her husband stood up and wrapped his arm around her. 'Thank you all so much for coming. It means a lot. A lot.' He sat back down, drawing Mrs Rakoff back into the seat next to him.

Mr Tollefsen, who'd been Eve, Jess and Kyle's fifth-grade teacher, stood up next. He talked about how curious Kyle was, how interested in everything around him. Ben Flood told a long, rambling story about playing football with Kyle.

When Ben sat down, Dave Perry got up. 'I think I'm the last person who saw Kyle alive.' He cleared his throat twice. 'I want everyone to know, he was happy. We were joking around.' Dave gave a choked laugh. 'He was just being Kyle, you know? He was a great friend.'

Jess squeezed Eve's hand. Eve squeezed back. More people stood to share their memories of Kyle, and Eve wondered if she should say anything. She'd known him for years, and they'd been lab partners. But she couldn't think about Kyle without remembering their last conversation. She wasn't like Dave. She didn't have good memories of the last time she saw Kyle. She'd been mean to him.

Eve was surprised when Briony stood to take a turn. 'I hardly knew Kyle,' she admitted, 'but he was the friendliest guy. He was the first person who talked to me on my first day. He took me on a tour of the school.' She gave a little smile. 'Not a normal one. He didn't show me where the office was or the cafeteria. But he showed me where the security cameras are, and where people go to make out.' She winced. 'Maybe I shouldn't have said that. What I wanted to say was, Kyle made me feel really welcome at Deepdene High. I wish I'd gotten a chance to get to know him better.' She sat down quickly.

Eve started to stand, but Helena beat her to it. She walked up to the front of the congregation with her head held high and tears running down her cheeks.

'Kyle was my true love,' she said. 'I would say he was my first true love, except that makes it sound like there will be others. There won't. I won't ever love anyone like I loved Kyle. We would have been together for ever if things had been different with Kyle.'

A long moment of silence followed Helena's words. Eve didn't want to risk breaking the quiet so instead she had an eye-conversation with Jess. Eve's eyes: *And he was just asking me out for coffee.* Jess's eyes: *I'm glad she doesn't know he didn't feel the same way about her.*

Bradley Rakoff, Kyle's older brother, stood up. 'Kyle used to follow me around all the time when he was little. It's like he wanted to be me. He'd knock on the doors of my friends' houses and ask if they could play, even though he was, like, five, and we were thirteen.' Bradley shook his head. 'It was as annoying as hell.' He wiped his eyes with his sleeve. 'But how many times are you loved that way?' He looked like he might say something else, but he sat down instead and buried his face against his mother's shoulder.

Eve decided not to speak. It felt like what Bradley had said should be the last statement. Everyone else seemed to feel the same way. Reverend Thompson announced the number of the closing hymn.

After they sang, Kyle's pall-bearers slowly carried his coffin out of the church. Pew by pew, everyone followed them. Eve blinked as she stepped out into the sunshine of the church courtyard. Somehow it seemed as if it should be dark out – or at least cloudy.

Luke walked over to her and Jess. 'Intense.'

They both nodded. What else was there to add?

'Did you hear anything more? With your dad being with Kyle's family,' Jess asked. 'I'm not asking for a gossip exchange,' she added, blushing.

'I know that,' Luke told her. 'You're worried. We're all worried.'

Eve put her arm around Jess's shoulders to comfort her.

'I haven't really heard much,' Luke went on. 'But the reason Kyle's casket was closed was because his wounds were too severe for the mortician to do much with them. I also saw in the paper this morning – and this is freaky – that his body had been totally drained of blood.'

'That's what I heard that day in the principal's office,' Jess said.

'The even weirder part was that there apparently wasn't much blood on the ground or anything. His blood was just . . . gone.'

'And they still don't know what did it,' Eve said. 'On the news this morning they had an animal expert. She said there was no known animal that could have caused the bites and claw marks on Kyle's body.' Jess wrapped her arms tightly around herself at Eve's words.

'Kyle's parents were pretty convinced it was wild dogs, so the bites would have been from at least a couple of different animals,' Luke said. 'But they talked to that same expert, and she ruled out any type of dog bite. None of the experts – the medical examiner, that animal woman, the cops – have come up with something that really fits.'

'You thought the police and animal control would be able to figure it out,' Eve reminded Luke, 'but they haven't. Do we still think nothing *extreme* was involved?'

'I saw that woman on TV too. She said there was no known animal on Earth that could have caused Kyle's injuries,' Jess said. 'Not on *Earth*.'

'And the police didn't come up with another theory

– like some kind of weapon that could have caused the wounds,' Luke added.

They looked at each other. 'So not an animal, not a human weapon . . . but there is another possibility.' Eve didn't want to say it aloud, but she knew they were all thinking the same thing. 'Kyle could have been killed by . . .'

They all finished together. 'A demon.'

Chapter Four

'OK, now we can *talk* talk,' Eve said. She, Jess and Luke had gotten some coffee from the pot that had been set out on a table in the church courtyard, then found a secluded spot over in a nook by the rectory.

'Maybe we're jumping to conclusions,' Jess said. 'I mean, someone can have Tori Burch shoes but still carry a purse from the American Signature collection.'

Luke's brow furrowed in confusion, so Eve handled the translation. 'You can wear legitimate designer shoes and still be carrying a knock-off handbag. By which I'd say Jess means we have had legitimate demon encounters, but that doesn't mean we are dealing with a demon this time. Even if it *looks* like a demon, that doesn't make it one.'

'Right. Maybe those animals with the weird migration patterns also have strange mutations.

Mutations no one has recorded yet. Weird teeth that leave weird bite marks. The ability to suck out all a person's blood,' Jess said, clearly trying to convince herself it was true.

'Reporter sighting. To the left.' It was the same man Luke had seen at Ola's. 'He's not close enough to hear us though.'

'In the offensive trench coat and the cowboy boots?' Jess asked.

Luke nodded, then looked over at Eve. 'Even *I* can see that coat needs burning. But no fires,' he teased.

Jess gave the reporter a disgusted look. 'I know those boots must be a huge temptation too, more than the coat even. But I agree with Luke. No fires. You've got to keep your secret superpowers secret.'

'Hey, I have a pair of boots almost exactly like his. I've worn them to school. Why didn't you two tell me I was a walking what-not-to-wear?' Luke demanded, acting like he was offended, but clearly also trying not to smile.

Eve turned so her back was to the boot-wearing reporter. 'So what do you guys think I should I be doing with my superpowers?' she asked her friends. 'Like Jess said, we don't know that we're dealing with a you-know-what. But, in a town that used to be called Demondene, a place where a demon was going to school with us a few weeks ago, we need to give it some consideration. We need to be prepared.'

'Do you think Malphas could be back?' Luke asked.

'I don't know if I killed him exactly,' Eve answered. 'I mean, maybe he's immortal. But I don't think he's anywhere around here any more.'

'He's as gone as hair scrunchies,' Jess agreed. 'He went up in smoke, and his whole mansion crumbled.' Mal had taken over the old Razor place near the beach and completely renovated it. When Eve smoked him, the mansion reverted to the ruin it had been, complete with wild jungle of a garden.

Eve frowned. 'Although I did smell wood-smoke the night of that charity thing down on the beach – after he was gone. And again that day you were helping me with my powers. Mal and his demon buddies always smelled like wood-smoke. I thought all his minions disappeared with Mal. Do you think I could have missed one? Could that be what killed Kyle?'

Jess shook her head. 'Completely different MO. Mal basically kissed people to suck out their soul, and the victims didn't die – they just became insane.'

'Until Evie got Mal to vomit the souls back up. Don't forget that part,' Luke said. 'We won last time. If we have to fight a demon again, we'll win again.'

'But even if we do, I won't be able to save Kyle. He's being buried right now.' Eve could see Kyle's family gathering graveside in the small cemetery next to the church. They'd asked that the burial be private. Eve gripped her coffee so tightly that the cardboard cup buckled, sloshing the hot liquid onto her new coat with the asymmetrical flounced hem.

'Get that directly to the dry-cleaners,' Jess said, eyeing the spot.

'Yeah,' Eve agreed, her eyes still on the cemetery, her thoughts still on Kyle. The man in the trench coat was looking over there too, watching as Kyle's mother sobbed. Eve felt a stab of anger. 'That reporter is a ghoul,' she muttered. 'How can he stand having a job where all he does is skulk around grieving people, trying to sniff out some news? Go home, Trench!'

Jess nodded. 'Yeah! And take your ugly boots with you.'

The guy in the trench coat was too far away to hear them. He didn't glance away from the graveyard.

'OK, let's think it through, and somebody warn me if Trench comes this way,' Luke said, half joking, half serious. 'We have the wood-smoke smell, a death that doesn't match any known animals, even though it looks like an animal attack . . . anything else?'

Eve considered the question for a moment, then shook her head.

'So first up we need to figure out what we're dealing with. That means research,' Luke said. 'I still haven't finished translating all the papers we found in the church. I should have kept working on it, but once Mal was dealt with I let it slide.'

Reverend Simon, who'd been Deepdene Church's minister before Luke's dad, had given clues in his journal about where the papers with information vital to destroying Malphas could be found.

'Do you think those papers would even have anything about other demons?' Jess asked. 'Reverend Simon only wrote about a master demon that would return every hundred years – and that was Malphas.'

'The papers were from all over, some of them written centuries ago,' Luke replied. 'I didn't find anything in the parts I read that seemed to be about a different kind of demon, but who knows what other information could be in them? If the men who wrote about Malphas knew about other demons, it makes sense they'd include the info.'

'There's also the Internet,' Eve said. She shifted her body towards Luke so that she couldn't see the graveyard. 'That's where you found out about the first Deepdene Witch, Luke.' Eve's brow furrowed. 'Sometimes I still can't believe I'm her descendant.' She shook her head. 'So, research this weekend?'

'Dyeah,' Jess said. It was one of the first words they'd come up with together, a combo of 'duh' and 'yeah'.

'Dyeah,' Luke agreed.

'You don't even know what you're saying,' Jess accused him. 'Dyeah' was part of Eve and Jess's best-friend vocab, and outsiders didn't speak that language.

'Duh, yeah, I do,' Luke answered. 'It doesn't exactly require a code breaker to understand you two.'

Eve knew that was true. The words weren't even supposed to be code. They were just shorthand, or words for things that should already have words but didn't. Luke was the first person to ever jump in and start using the words too, like they belonged to him as well. *I guess demon hunting together creates a bond that's almost like the one between BFFs*, she decided.

'When we meet up, you should get in some more practice time on your powers,' Luke told Eve. 'You were awesome that night against Mal, but—'

'But I'm not exactly in control.'

'Yeah. Ask my jacket,' Luke joked.

'That night I was so scared and angry.' She didn't mention the strange attraction to Mal that had almost overcome her, even after she'd realized he was a demon. That wasn't something she wanted to share with anyone. It was too strange, too unsettling. 'And the power just came out. Whoosh.'

'I know you can learn to pull the trigger whenever you need to, no matter how you're feeling. You just need to practise,' Luke said.

'Until then, I always know how to make you mad,' Jess added. 'I can help you practise by borrowing your lip gloss.' She looked over at Luke. 'FYI, that always makes her go mental, in case you need her powers fast.'

'Good to know, even though I only wear lip gloss on special occasions,' Luke said.

'Until we deal with this new demon – if it even is a demon – I'm going to need you to stay close,' Eve told Luke. 'No one makes me as mad as fast as you do, lipstick or not.'

'Not a problem. Whenever you need me to enrage you, I'll be there,' Luke promised. His tone was light, but his green eyes were serious. She really could count on him. She knew that in her gut.

'Me too,' Jess said.

'You two are the best,' Eve told them. 'The absolute best.'

'True,' Luke answered. 'Also, I figure that the safest place to be with a demon around is with the Deepdene Witch.'

Before Eve could reply, her mom called to her from the church steps. 'Eve, we need to get going.'

'OK,' Eve called back. She turned to her friends. 'I'll text you about getting together.'

'Demon, prepare to have your ass kicked,' Jess said. 'Or do you think there might be more than one?'

'Maybe there's not one at all,' Luke replied. 'But it doesn't matter. Road-tripping mountain lion, mutant dog, demon – we can handle the kicking of any of those asses.'

'Eve,' her mother called again. Patience wasn't high on her list of virtues.

'Gotta go,' Eve told Jess and Luke. 'Bye.' She hurried across the courtyard towards her parents, but something made her pause. She wanted to see Luke's face one more time before she left. Somehow, when the madness got going, he made her feel strong. She glanced over her shoulder – and found him already looking at her.

His expression was gripping, sending a quiver through her body from head to toe. Eve found it hard to turn away from his intense gaze. She tore her eyes away from him, but her mind was whirling.

What on earth was that? she wondered.

Chapter Five

'Substitute in math. Ms T is out,' Ben told Luke as they passed each other in the hall before last period on Thursday, almost a week after Kyle's funeral.

Cool, Luke thought. Ms Taylor could be kind of a hardass. It would be a nice break to have a sub. Often, a sub meant a chance to get some homework done in class. That would free up time after school to keep working on translating the papers that had been hidden in the church. It had been more than a week since Kyle was killed, and Luke still hadn't found anything useful on the new demon, if a demon was what they were dealing with.

There hadn't been any more attacks, so he was starting to hope it had been some kind of strange animal, maybe one that was lost and hurt and scared and so it attacked Kyle before it crawled off onto the beach and got washed away.

It didn't seem likely.

There were still a lot of Latin pages to get through. Somewhere in them could be some vital info. Even though Luke's dad had insisted that Luke start studying Latin in elementary school – he claimed it was the basis of pretty much everything – it was still taking for ever to work his way through the material.

Eve was already in her seat when he walked into the room for math. He flopped down at the desk across the aisle from her. Ms Taylor wasn't a hardass about stuff like who sat where, just about turning in homework on time and actually learning the material. You got behind in Ms T's class and you started getting private tutoring from her, whether you wanted it or not.

'Hey,' Luke said to Eve, glancing at the sub, who was standing awkwardly at the front of the room, waiting for the bell to ring. She didn't seem to know what to do with her hands, putting them in her pockets, then clasping them behind her, then almost immediately pressing them against her sides. Most subs were a little nervous, but this one seemed like she was ready to bolt from the room.

'Do we look that scary?' Eve whispered.

'You do,' Luke answered.

Eve automatically reached up to smooth her hair. Luke smiled, until he noticed the scorch mark on the side of her hand. 'How did you do that?' he asked. The bell hadn't rung yet to start class, but this wasn't a conversation anyone else should be hearing. 'Was it . . . ?' He wiggled his fingers, pantomiming power shooting out.

'Kind of,' Eve admitted. 'I was *practising*, and I accidentally set my bed frame on fire. Just a little section. I got this' – she flexed her hand – 'putting it out. I think I'm going to move all future sessions to the bathtub.'

'At least you're getting a little control. Were you . . . *emotional* when you lit up the bed frame?' Luke had the urge to reach over and try to smooth away the burn mark with his fingers. Or maybe it was just the urge to touch her.

'No. I'm getting a handle on doing it cold. But it still takes way too long,' Eve replied. 'How's it going on your side? Find out anything?'

'No. Some old parish papers are mixed in with the other stuff. I spent last night translating what ended up being a sermon about sloth,' Luke answered.

James Frankel dropped into the seat in front of

Luke. They would have to continue this particular conversation later.

'I can't believe Ms Taylor's out,' James commented. 'She seems like the type who would just refuse to get sick.'

'Yeah, hard to imagine her bowing down to some random bacteria,' Luke agreed. Eve frowned. 'What?' he asked.

'Ms Taylor's car was in the parking lot before school. At least, I'm pretty sure it was.' Her cheeks turned a little pink. 'Jess and I say good morning to it sometimes, because it's so cute. I want a Mini Cooper.'

'You don't have a licence,' James reminded her.

'I want one just to sit in,' Eve explained. 'I do think I saw her car today. I guess it could have been yesterday, but I can really picture it this morning.'

'When you stopped to talk to it,' Luke teased.

'Hey, Ms McHugh,' James called out, reading her name off the board. The sub started. 'What's up with Ms Taylor?'

'I . . . I don't know the details,' Ms McHugh answered.

Luke thought she was lying. Being a minister's son had given him a fairly accurate lie detector; people always lied to his dad, trying to pretend they were better behaved than they actually were. Ms McHugh was probably lying because there was a rule about subs giving out personal teacher info, even just something like, 'She has the flu.'

'Ms Taylor's car is outside,' Eve said.

'I don't know anything about that,' Ms McHugh said. 'All I know is she didn't call the office to let them know she wouldn't be here, and she didn't leave any lesson plans.' She bit her lip as if she hadn't planned to tell them that.

There was a rush of people through the door, just beating the bell. Ms McHugh scurried behind the desk and pulled out the clipboard Ms Taylor used for the attendance sheets. As she started calling names, Eve leaned across the aisle. 'I don't like this,' she said.

'Maybe she got here, wasn't feeling well and one of the other teachers drove her home,' Luke suggested. 'Except then the office would have known.'

'Do you think . . . ?'

Eve didn't finish the sentence, but Luke knew what she was asking. 'I think we'd better pick up the pace on the research.'

When Ms McHugh finished calling roll, Luke tapped Eve lightly on the arm. 'Follow my lead,' he said under his breath. He raised his hand. The sub pointed at him. 'Yes?'

'My study partner, Eve, and I are working on a special project.' He could practically feel his brain clicking as he tried to come up with a project involving math that would require the library. 'We're writing a report on the origins of algebra in Babylonia.' Jess wasn't the only one who watched the Discovery Channel. 'Could we get a library pass to work on it?'

'It's for extra credit,' Eve added smoothly. 'Ms Taylor lets us go to the library every Thursday.'

No one in the class laughed or called them on the lie. Luke was sure they were all wishing they'd come up with as brilliant a story.

Ms McHugh hesitated. 'Fine,' she decided. 'We're just going to have a study period in here anyway.'

'We need a pass. Ms Taylor keeps them in the top drawer,' Eve said. Ms McHugh quickly signed two passes and handed them over. Luke and Eve rushed out of the room before she could ask any more questions.

'Babylonia. Nice,' Eve said when he had shut the classroom door behind them.

'I don't have any of the demon papers with me, but

we can go online and keep looking for a demon whose attack style matches whatever killed Kyle,' Luke told her.

'There was an article in the *National Enquirer* yesterday that said it was chimps that had human DNA mixed with their own. Supposedly they escaped a lab and have now been sighted in Central Park.'

'Chimps do have sharp teeth,' Luke said as they started for the library, 'but the *Enquirer* isn't exactly a reliable source. It's up there with . . .'

Eve put a hand on his arm. 'Shhh. Is that someone crying?'

Luke listened. 'I think so.'

'It's coming from down there.' Eve jerked her chin towards the corridor leading down to the art rooms and the main office. She and Luke looked at each other for a moment, then changed course, following the sound of the soft sobs.

'She stayed late a lot,' someone said. 'What if someone grabbed her on her way to her car last night? It's too dark out there. I should have waited to go until she was ready to leave.' Luke recognized the voice. Mrs Ollestad, the school secretary. He'd spent some time with her when he'd registered as the new kid at the beginning of the semester.

He slowed his pace. Eve did too. They stopped a few feet before they reached the open door to the reception area.

'It's not your fault, Amanda. Don't even think that. I want you to go home and relax. I just need you to look up her emergency contact first. Can you do that? The police need to speak to her next of kin.' Another familiar voice – Principal Allison.

'Yes,' Mrs Ollestad answered. There was a quaver in her voice, but she'd stopped crying.

'What do you think has happened?' Eve whispered.

Luke thought she knew. The same way he thought he knew. It was just that neither of them wanted to say it aloud. Luke forced the words out. 'I think they're talking about Ms Taylor. I think she's dead.'

Chapter Six

Eve pressed her back against the wall. She needed it to prop her up. Her legs felt boneless, completely unable to keep her upright. Ms Taylor was dead. *Dead.* Eve felt the blood draining from her face at the thought.

Her fingertips began to prickle and she felt static electricity whisper through her hair. Her body was preparing for battle, even though whatever had killed Ms Taylor wasn't near enough to zap.

Luke wrapped an arm around her, and Eve turned and buried her face in his chest. His warm body supported her so, so much better than the cool hard wall. She put her arms around his back and held on tight. The comfort of being that close to him helped keep her powers from flying out of control. For a few moments they just stood and breathed together.

I'm standing here hugging Luke. The thought startled her and she jumped away from him. 'That was . . .' She wasn't sure what word went there. Nice? Awkward? Comforting? Awkward? Hot? Awkward?

'Yeah.' Luke said the word to his shoes. Then he looked up at her and they both kind of laughed. 'Yeah, that was . . .' Eve waited to hear what word he'd use. 'It was . . . that. Let's get out of here.'

Eve nodded, and they walked over to one of the side entrances. They both acted like they had permission to leave as they stepped out into the crisp fall air and kept walking – not too fast – across the fallen leaves in the quad and down the street.

'Ms Taylor . . .' Eve began. 'Whatever killed Kyle is still out there.'

'I know.'

They continued in silence, making their way over to Main Street. 'Hot chocolate?' Luke suggested as they approached Java Nation.

'Perfect,' Eve answered. 'Hot chocolate is my go-to beverage of comfort.'

Luke opened the door for her. 'Which is why I asked,' he said.

'You knew that? Why do you know that?' she asked.

'I realize that we haven't known each other very long, Evie, but we have been in a bunch of situations that required hot chocolate,' Luke said.

'And here we are again.' Eve let out a sigh. 'Hot chocolate central.'

'I'll get our drinks.' Luke said.

Eve chose a table in the corner, one that wasn't easy to see through the big front windows. After all, she and Luke had cut last period. 'Whipped cream!' she called as Luke stepped up to the counter.

He gave her a tell-me-something-I-don't-know eye roll. Eve smiled. Somehow, even with the badness that had clearly invaded Deepdene, being with Luke could still make her smile. Eve idly rubbed at the scorch mark on her hand. The burn wasn't bad, but looking at it bothered her. It had taken way too long to shoot out the bolts of fire that torched her bed frame. In fact, she'd actually given up any hope of switching her power on. She wouldn't have been aiming at the bed frame if she'd thought she'd been *live.* She'd flopped down on the bed, arms flung up over her head, then – *zap.* Not good.

She was getting better though. Before the bed-frame incident she'd managed to light a few candles. No melting. No exploding.

'Double whipped cream,' Luke announced as he set the big cup in front of Eve and sat down across from her.

Eve swiped her finger across the whipped cream, then licked it off. She loved to have one taste of the whipped cream straight up, before she let it mix with the chocolate.

'Can I have a taste?' Luke opened his mouth, like he expected her to hold out a fingerful of whipped cream for him to lick.

Luke's a flirt, Eve reminded herself. *He flirts with everyone. He can't help himself. Doesn't mean a thing.*

'You want a bite, go ask for a spoon. Even better, ask for your own whipped cream,' Eve told him. She shook her head. 'I *really* hope that wasn't your A game.'

'Not even close. When you see it, you won't have to ask,' Luke joked. He took a notebook out of his backpack and flipped it open. 'We need to come up with a way to get more details about Kyle and Ms Taylor's deaths. We've got to find out what we're dealing with.'

'But we don't even know for sure that she's dead,' Eve said. But her gut really, really knew. 'We don't know what happened. They didn't say anything about an animal attack, or even that they found her body. Maybe she's only missing.'

'You don't believe that, and neither do I,' Luke said. 'Ms Taylor's body . . .'

Eve put a hand on his wrist, stopping him. She tilted her head to the right.

'Trench. Perfect,' he muttered, catching on.

The reporter stood across the street, talking on his cell. He didn't look as if he had taken off his coat since they saw him at Kyle's funeral almost a week before. It was even more rumpled and stained than it had been then. And it seemed like he hadn't shaved since then either. The stubble on his face was thick and dark.

'Do you think he knows?' Eve asked softly. 'About Ms Taylor?'

'No,' Luke decided. 'If he knew, he'd already be at school, sniffing around, hoping he'd find someone to give him the gory details.'

'The details we want,' Eve reminded him, her eyes still on Trench.

'We want them so we can help. Not to sell a story.'

'He's coming this way,' Eve said. Trench had started across the street. 'Let's leave. I don't want him asking us how everyone at school is dealing with Kyle's death.'

Luke stood and grabbed his coffee. Eve picked up her hot chocolate. They hurried out of Java Nation.

'I'd say we should just go hang at my house,' Eve said. 'Probably neither of my parents is home right now. But some of our neighbours are very chatty. I can just see one of them asking my mom why I was out of school early this afternoon.'

They turned the corner, leaving Main Street, and meandered down the sidewalk as they sipped their drinks. 'Try being the minister's kid. People love to tell my dad everything I do,' Luke said. 'Probably at church this Sunday someone will ask my dad if he approves of my drinking coffee at my age.'

'It must be hard for him to have a son that's so out of control,' Eve kidded.

'You said it.'

Eve's iPhone buzzed. 'Message from Jess,' she told Luke. She held it up to him so he could read it: WHERE R U? BAD NEWS.

Eve shot out a reply: MS T? I KNOW. WITH LUKE. MEET AT MINE IN 10?

Her friend sent back an 'OK' almost instantly. 'Jess is going to meet me at my house,' she told Luke. 'Want to come?'

'I should go home. The papers from the church might have some key information, and I want to keep translating,' Luke said.

Eve felt a little pang of what felt like disappointment. She'd just assumed Luke would come with her. But his plan made sense. 'Jess and I will hit the computer and see what we can find out.' *I'm not disappointed*, she decided. *I see Luke all the time. I guess I'm just a little worried about walking home by myself.*

Not that she had far to go alone. She and Luke went in the same direction most of the way. Eve only had to walk about a block by herself, and when she was halfway down that block she spotted Jess on the porch waiting for her. Eve picked up her pace, and Jess hurried down the porch steps and out Eve's front gate. When they met on the sidewalk Eve gave her friend a tight hug.

'Oh my God, Eve,' Jess said as they headed into the house. 'I just – oh my God.'

'I know,' Eve agreed. 'What did they say about Ms Taylor at school? Did Principal Allison make an announcement? Luke and I overheard her and Mrs Ollestad talking. That's how we found out something had happened to her. She's dead, isn't she?'

'Yeah,' Jess answered. 'The principal went from class to class telling people Ms Taylor's body had been found. She didn't give any details, just tried to keep everyone from losing it.'

Eve and Jess went directly to the living room. Eve grabbed the remote and clicked on the TV. 'We didn't hear the specifics either.' A couple more clicks and she saw the image of their school. Ms Taylor's death had reached the news. People were milling about in front of the main steps as the reporter spoke to the camera. Eve sat down on the couch next to Jess.

'. . . confirmed to be Ms Jill Taylor,' the TV reporter was saying. 'Her body was discovered by Allen Hodges of Amagansett, who was walking his dog in the Deepdene woods, very near where the body of Deepdene High student Kyle Rakoff was found last week. The wounds on Taylor's body are very similar to those suffered by Rakoff, according to early reports from the chief of police. Bites and claw marks were present, and her body had been completely drained of blood.'

Eve and Jess exchanged a look. 'The same thing got Ms Taylor that got Kyle.' Jess's voice shook as she said the words. Eve nodded, then returned her attention to the TV.

'The cause of Taylor's and Rakoff's wounds has yet to be determined. While they appear to have been the victims of some kind of animal attack, forensics specialists haven't been able to match a specific animal to the bite and claw marks. Additionally, search parties made up of the local police and concerned citizens have been attempting to find the animal – whatever it may be – without success.'

'Cos they're looking for an animal,' Eve said. She was becoming more and more convinced that there was a supernatural being behind the murders. Maybe a demon, maybe something else, but nothing *normal.*

'The police are investigating possible connections between Taylor and Rakoff. Rakoff was not one of Taylor's students, but in a school the size of Deepdene High it is very likely they have had some contact.'

The front door flew open so fast that it hit the wall with a bang. Eve and Jess both jumped.

Eve's father was out of breath, and he looked relieved to see them. 'Eve, you're here. And Jess too. Good. Neither of you should be alone. I left the office as soon as I heard.' He closed the door more gently. 'Sorry about that. Didn't mean to scare you.'

He sat down on the couch next to Eve and glanced at the television. 'Look at those vultures.' More reporters had joined the scene. Eve spotted Trench among them. They were all trying to find students and teachers who would talk to them.

'Doesn't sound like there's any new information,' her dad said as the reporter began repeating the basic facts again. 'Your parents know you're here, don't they?' he asked Jess.

'Yup,' Jess said.

'Good. Otherwise they'd be frantic.' He looked at Eve. 'Your mom's on her way home too.'

'Mom's coming home early?' Eve asked in surprise. Both her parents had high-powered jobs. She hardly ever had both of them home in time for dinner, although they tried hard to make sure one of them was.

'She's worried. Two deaths in two weeks in our little town. With no real idea what's happened.' He shook his head, then got up. 'I'm making my famous mac and cheese. You staying, Jess? You're very welcome.'

'Thanks, Mr Evergold. That would be great,' Jess called after him as he headed for the kitchen.

Eve clicked the TV off. 'We can check in a little while to see if they've figured out anything new. We should hit the computer and keep looking for creatures that match the attacks, even though we don't have super-detailed information.'

'What key words should we try this time?' Eve asked when they were up in her bedroom, settled at the computer. At least her power surges were more under control. She'd stopped shorting out electronics, which she'd done almost non-stop for the first few weeks after her Deepdene Witch powers had manifested.

'How about . . . "demon attack with bites"?' Jess suggested.

Eve typed the words into Google and started skimming through the results. 'A lot of these deal with the mysterious appearance of bite marks on a person. Claw marks too. But I'm not seeing anything where the attack was so bad that somebody died.' She tapped her fingers lightly on the keyboard. 'I'm going to try "supernatural deaths".'

'Sometimes I can't believe we're doing the things we do,' Jess said. 'Like this. Trying to identify what supernatural being is murdering people in our town.'

'I know.' Eve scanned the new results. 'The whole first page is all about that show *Supernatural*. There was an episode called "Death Takes a Holiday".' She clicked to go to the next page. 'More stuff about the show.'

Jess peered over Eve's shoulder. 'It's telling us we could also try "*mysterious* supernatural deaths",' she pointed out.

'Is there any other kind?' Eve started the new

search. 'Here's one about a hospital where every patient who was in a certain bed on a Friday morning – every Friday morning – died.'

'Creepy. Any bites or claw marks?'

'No.' Eve gave a snort of disgust. 'It says when the hospital set up surveillance they saw a cleaning woman go into the room and unplug the life-support system so she could plug in the vacuum.'

'That sounds like an urban legend. Not helpful,' Jess said.

'So not helpful, and so stupid,' Eve agreed. She returned to the results. More stuff about *Supernatural* the show. Some entries about the movie *The Grudge.* Didn't anyone care about real life?

'Oooh. Here's a blog about supernatural stuff.' Jess tapped the screen, and Eve clicked on the link. Which, for some bizarre reason, took them to a site with a list of local dry-cleaners.

'You don't think *something* is trying to stop us from finding out what we need to know, do you?' Jess asked.

'I don't think a demon has taken possession of my computer so it can keep us from searching the Net, if that's what you're asking.'

'It was. And you never know,' Jess said.

'Eve, Jess, dinner!' Eve's mom called before Eve could reply.

'It's just the Internet as usual,' Eve said. 'You always get weird hits when you do a search. Nothing supernatural about that.'

'Yeah. I guess it's just when there's some weird, horrible thing going on, *everything* starts to feel weird and horrible.'

'True that,' Eve agreed.

When they stepped into the dining room, the table was perfectly set, with salad forks and lit candles and everything. Eve's family never did this for a regular-night dinner. And it wasn't as if Jess counted as company. She was there way too much for that. Eve's place was her second home, and vice versa.

But this isn't a regular night, Eve realized. *It's a night after a scary freaky thing happened. The second scary freaky thing in a really short time.*

Eve's mom came in carrying a big wooden bowl of salad. Eve spotted cranberries, feta, walnuts. Her mother had gone all out in the salad area too. Maybe turning into Martha Stewart was helping her deal with everything.

'Looks good, Mrs Evergold,' Jess said, taking her usual seat.

'It really does. Thanks, Mom,' Eve added. She sat down next to Jess.

'Your father did the heavy lifting. He made his legendary mac and cheese,' Eve's mother said with a wink.

'And nobody try to get the recipe out of me. It's a secret,' her dad said. He carried the gigantic steaming serving dish into the dining room and set it down on the table with a flourish. 'Only when I die will I pass it on to you,' he told Eve.

Eve gave a snort of laughter. But in a way death was too close tonight. Not something to joke about.

Her mother served herself some of the salad. 'You girls went to see that new vampire movie last week-end, didn't you?' She didn't wait for an answer. 'What did you think?'

And that's how the rest of the dinner conversation went. Safe topics. Eve didn't want the meal to end. But when it did, she and Jess went straight back to the computer.

Jess took the keyboard this time. 'I'm going to try "supernatural animal attacks".' She shook her head when hits came up. 'Mysterious attacks *on* animals is not what we're looking for, and I don't think we're dealing with Bigfoot. Although if demons exist, why not Bigfoot? Wait. Does Santa Claus?'

'Santa Claus absolutely exists,' Eve promised, smiling. 'I'm not sure about—'

Her phone rang. 'It's Luke,' she told Jess. She took the call. 'What's up?'

'I found out holy water burns demons. So that might be useful. I'm going to get some vials of it, so we'll always have some with us,' Luke said. 'That's it so far.'

'Better than us. We haven't found out anything yet,' Eve admitted. 'We'll keep looking though.'

'Me too,' Luke said. 'I guess I should get back to it. We've got to get a handle on what's going on.'

'Just so you know, Jess and I have decided that since demons are real, Santa is too,' Eve told him.

'Only fair,' Luke said. 'I guess I should get back to it.'

Eve didn't know if he'd forgotten he just said that or what. 'And me,' she said.

But Luke didn't say goodbye. Neither did she. They just sort of breathed together, the way they had when they were hugging in the hallway. It felt good being connected to him, even in such an insubstantial way. *What would it be like to kiss him?*

Where had that come from?! She didn't want to kiss Luke. Or, wait, did she?

'So, OK, well, bye,' Luke finally said.

'Bye.' Eve clicked off the phone and realized Jess was staring at her with raised eyebrows.

'What was that?' Jess asked.

'Luke wanted to let me know he hasn't found anything helpful in the stuff he's translating,' Eve said.

'So he basically called for nothing.' Jess's brows went a little higher. 'He luuurves you,' she announced.

'He luuurves half the girls at school,' Eve reminded her.

'No, he doesn't,' Jess said. 'My sources say he hasn't even gone out with anyone in two whole weeks. Not even Briony, and she's cute and new.'

'Two whole weeks? Wow!' Eve said sarcastically.

'Yes, wow – for Luke. That's like two months in player time,' Jess told her.

Eve laughed. 'Luke and I are friends. And he's been awesome helping with the demon stuff. But that's it.' Except she'd thought about kissing him.

'Haven't you noticed the way he looks at you?' Jess asked. 'He doesn't look at you like a guy looks at a friend, or even like a guy looks at a hot girl. It's luuurve, I'm telling you.'

Luke was extra sweet today, Eve thought. And it had felt so good snuggling up against his chest. Had it felt as good to him? He'd been trying to comfort her, but had something more been going on?

'You're thinking about it. You know I'm right,' Jess teased.

'I don't have time to think about my love life, not with everything that's going on,' Eve protested. 'I have to be ready to deal with . . . whatever it is that's happening. Remember, I'm the Deepdene Witch!'

'I say there's always time to think about boys, but it's your love life.' Jess turned back to the computer. 'Searching for animal attacks isn't working so well. But like you said, you're the Deepdene Witch. The first one – your Great-Great-Great-Grandmother Annabelle, I mean – was supposed to be obsessed with demons, and she fought them. If we can find out more about her, maybe it will help us.'

'That book Luke found on the Internet didn't have anything useful, but that doesn't mean there's nothing out there,' Eve said. 'Try looking up Annabelle Sewall and Demondene.'

Jess quickly typed in the words. 'Nothing,' she said. 'You hardly ever get *nothing*.' She tapped on the monitor. 'If anyone's in there, come out and I'll give you a cookie,' she said. 'Then you blast it,' she whispered to Eve.

'Maybe just try the name, but put in her middle name. It was Amelia,' Eve suggested.

'We just went from nothing to way too much,' Jess said as she started to scan the results. 'There's an Annabelle Amelia Sewall getting married. Getting promoted. Arrested. There's a book with a heroine named Annabelle Amelia, but it was written a couple of years ago and is set in Hollywood, so . . .' She scrolled through the pages, continuing to mutter to herself. 'Wait. This might be something. Her name is in another book, but a non-fiction one. It's a collection of writing from women's journals, starting in 1650, up to the present. There's an entry from an Annabelle Amelia Sewall. The year works too.'

'Has to be her!' Eve exclaimed.

'Dang it. It's on one of those research sites you have to pay for,' Jess said.

Eve grabbed her purse and whipped out her AmEx. Well, it was hers in that she used it; it was her parents' in that they paid the bills. A minute later they were on the site, and a scan of the excerpt from the diary of Eve's great-great-great-grandmother was on the screen. Eve leaned over Jess's shoulder and began to read:

20th of March

It has been twenty-five years to the day since my Percy died, and there are times I feel his loss as keenly as I did in those first days after the Evil took him from me. My Talents were not at their full. Nay, that is an untruth. I was not yet experienced enough to wield them with the skill I needed to save him. If it were today the Demon came and tried to wrench my beloved husband from me, I believe I would triumph.

It is foolish to ponder on such things. The past is done; regrets are futile. I must keep vigilant. I must be always attuned to the Darkness. I must continue to tend to my Talents, as when I do I continue to learn new ways they may be put to God's use. The limitations are in myself; I have found no limits in the Gift.

My Percy is gone. My time with him was much too brief, less even than one full cycle of the seasons. Yet there will always be others to protect, whom I may not love, who may fear and hate me, yet who deserve the safety my Gift, if that is what it is, can give them. On this day, a day that to me is all but sacred, I vow that I, Annabelle Amelia Sewell, will continue to be their champion against the Evil that so often manages to invade this village.

'That's so sad,' Eve said softly when she'd finished reading. 'Her husband died before they were even married a year.'

'Poor Annabelle. I wonder if she had even one friend. When your dad told us about her, it sounded like everyone in the village was scared of her, and she pretty much says that in her diary.'

'Well, she did wander around talking about demons all the time,' Eve answered. 'People knew she was obsessed with them. That limits your friend pool right there.'

'Don't worry. You can talk about demons as much as you want,' Jess told her. 'I'm not going anywhere.'

'Thanks.' Warmth filled Eve's body. The sensation was almost like her power coming to life. *Bestie Power*, she thought, smiling at her best friend. 'I wonder what else Annabelle learned to do with her power.'

'I know!' Jess exclaimed. 'She'd had her witch groove on for at least twenty-five years, since she had it when her husband died. And she said she was still figuring out new things she could do with her magic all those years later.' She twisted round in her chair and looked at Eve full on.

'What?' Eve said, when her friend wouldn't stop staring.

'Just thinking about what you might be able to do. I mean, we know your mojo can be used for other things than blasting way-too cute demonic creatures,' Jess said.

'We do?' Eve thought for a second. 'You mean lighting candles? There are easier ways to do that. Easier and a lot less messy!'

'Not candles, goofy. Remember when I was having those horrible nightmares because Mal's demons were trying to loosen up my soul for sucking?' Jess asked.

Eve was never, never going to forget the sight of her friend writhing in terror. 'Yeah, I remember.'

'You touched me, and it made the dreams go away. That's one of the other things you can do with your powers,' Jess said.

'It did feel different,' Eve admitted. 'Softer, somehow. More like waves coming out of me than a hard blast.'

'You have different settings. Like a blow-dryer or something.' Jess giggled, then her face went uncharacteristically serious. 'Who knows what you can really do, Eve? You've already done amazing things, but there might be so much more.'

Eve thought about the bright pool of power she knew was deep inside her. She thought Jess was right. She didn't know what it could really do. What *she* could really do.

Chapter Seven

'Let's start with some jumping jacks!' Vic cried, as if jumping jacks were the most exciting activity ever invented. The other cheerleaders obediently – but not quite as enthusiastically – followed instructions.

Eve smiled as she looked on from the bleachers by the football field. It was kind of fun watching other people exercise when you didn't have to. She hated getting sweaty at school.

Vic led the squad through an intense warm-up routine, then the girls gathered in little clusters. Eve climbed off the bleachers and headed over to Jess, Vic and Jenna. Eve and Jess were going to walk home together after Jess was finished with practice. It was a new school rule. No one left the grounds alone. It was buddy system all the way.

'What's up?' she asked her friends.

'Waiting on the coach,' Victoria answered. 'You

know she'd have a cow, a lamb and four squealing piggies if one of us showed up late.'

Jess laughed. 'So true.'

'Where is the coach anyway?' Rose Makishimia asked, joining the group.

'Still in her office. Our new uniforms came in, and there was a mistake in the order,' Vic said. 'Somewhere a customer-service agent is about to cry.'

'Good,' Rose answered. 'Not about the crying. But about where Coach Leonard is. I thought maybe . . .' She knotted her hands together.

Jenna gave an exaggerated shiver. 'I know. I keep wondering when it's going to happen again.'

'Not when,' Eve said. 'If.' Although when actually seemed more likely. Why would the creature – whatever it was – stop at two attacks?

'Right, if,' Jenna agreed. 'Although supposedly there's already been a third one.'

'Here?' Rose's voice came out as a high squeak.

Jenna nodded. 'You know Creepy?'

They said yes. Everyone in town knew Creepy. Or at least knew about her. She was this old woman who lived in a ramshackle mansion over on Elm. She never came out of the house, just got things delivered. All the little kids were scared of her. Some of the big kids too.

'Well, my older sister knows the guy who usually has to deliver her groceries. She makes him leave them on the porch. Anyway, the guy said a couple of days ago he went to her house with her usual order. She has it set up so she gets exactly the same order every week,' Jenna continued. 'As he was going up to the house, he supposedly smelled something terrible. Like rotting flesh.'

'Creepy?' Jess exclaimed.

Jenna looked annoyed at the interruption. 'No. But her groceries from the week before were still on the porch and all the meat had spoiled. The police are supposedly looking for her body right now. I'm sure the animal got her.'

Supposedly, Eve thought. To Eve, supposedly kind of meant: here's a big, fat rumour that's probably a big, fat lie.

'At my cousin's school – it's up in Syracuse – they've had an attack too. It was kind of like Kyle. She was heading home after her last class and never got there.' Vic lowered her voice. 'Her body had bite marks all over it too. The police in Syracuse think it might be a case of cannibalism.'

'Oh, eww!' Jess exclaimed.

'There are cannibals out there,' Vic said. 'Seriously.

I heard there was an ad on Craigslist from this man looking for a woman to cut out some meat from his calf and then serve it for dinner. He wanted to cannibalize himself!'

Rose screwed up her face. 'That is beyond disgusting.'

'I'm thinking it's also beyond true,' Eve commented. At least she really, really hoped so. That was just foul.

'Maybe. Maybe not,' Vic answered.

'Go back to Creepy,' Rose said to Jenna. 'What—'

Jenna cut her off. 'Where's the coach? She can't still be cursing at customer service. It's giving me the creeps that she's not here yet.' She rubbed her arms with her hands.

'What if something got her between the school and the field?' Rose said. 'You know, something . . .' She curled her fingers into claws and scratched them through the air.

'I'll go check,' Eve volunteered. In another minute the cheerleaders might get a case of mass hysteria going. Besides, if the creature was roaming around school, Eve was the only one who might have a chance of coming face to face with it and surviving.

She cut across the football field, heading for the

school building. It wasn't too far way. As she circled around the bleachers opposite where she'd been sitting, she heard a shriek. She whipped back towards the field – and saw all the cheerleaders running towards her. Not jogging or trotting. Running full out. Squealing, shouting, crying, howling.

'Is it still back there?' one of the girls yelled.

'I don't know, I don't know, just get inside!' Jenna shouted back.

Jess grabbed Eve's arm as the crowd surged past. She kept racing for the school, pulling Eve with her. 'What happened?' Eve cried.

'It had a face!' Jess exclaimed, running faster. Eve stumbled, trying to keep up.

'Wait. That's the guys' locker room!' Eve yelled.

Too late. Victoria had already shoved the door open and the cheerleaders rampaged through, Jess still clinging tightly to Eve's arm.

'I knew this day would come,' Eli Belfer called. He had on his sweatshirt and a pair of boxers with red and pink kisses. His feet were bare. 'I've dreamed about it!'

Luke rushed over. 'What's going on?' He tightened the knot on the drawstring of his grey sweatpants. His chest was bare.

'The animal – it's out there. The one that killed Kyle and Ms Taylor!' Vic burst out.

'It wasn't even . . . It had a face!' Jess added. She kept saying that. Eve wasn't even sure what she meant.

'Girls, girls. You didn't have to make up a story to come in here,' Bill Salvatore told them. 'We understand that you've been dying for a peek.'

'No, it was real,' Victoria told him. 'If we wanted a peek, we would have gone to the nearest college, where the guys have actually matured.'

'You really saw something?' Dave asked from a bench in front of one of the lockers. His face looked almost grey, and Eve knew he was thinking about Kyle.

'Yes!' three or four of the girls answered at once.

Eve knew that she had to get back out there. Her eyes met Luke's, and a second later they were running from the locker room.

'I'm coming!' Jess called, racing after them. It sounded like the whole football team and all the cheerleaders were coming too.

'Where was it?' Eve cried, her hair whipping across her face as she ran.

'Down by the far goalpost,' Jess answered. 'Be careful,' she added as they tore across the grass. 'It's huge.

Huge as a horse. But furry like a dog. And with a face!'

Luke skidded to a halt at the goalpost and started scanning the area. Eve and Jess stopped next to him and started looking around too. 'Is it gone? I think it might be gone,' Jess said breathlessly.

'Maybe all that squealing and screaming scared it off,' Luke joked. 'It scared me a little when you came into the locker room.'

Eve glanced over at him, and her eyes snagged on his broad shoulders and tight abs. He was seriously hot. *So not the time*, she told herself, forcing her gaze away from his bare chest. She turned in a slow circle, looking for the creature. Everybody else was wandering the field searching for the beast too.

'You said it was as big as a horse, but hairy like a dog?' Luke asked Jess. He sounded doubtful.

'Uh-huh,' Jess answered. 'And it had this horrible face. Not a dog face. A little like a monkey's. And its eyes were red!'

Supposedly, Eve suddenly thought. 'Jess, do you think . . . ? We were kind of freaking each other out with those stories about Creepy and the cannibals. Do you think maybe you guys just saw a regular dog, a big one, but since you were already scared you—'

'No,' Jess said firmly. 'It wasn't a dog.'

'There's nothing out here,' Bill called from partway down the field. 'It's like I said. They wanted a look at our chiselled bodies, but they were too shy to say so.'

'I'm not shy,' Jenna answered loudly. She reached over and pinched his butt. 'He does have nice glutes,' she added.

'Does anyone want to test mine?' Eli shouted. 'My butt is available for pinching, squeezing, whatever. Just form a line. No shoving. Everyone will get a turn.'

'It really was here,' Jess said to Eve and Luke. 'And it wasn't . . . It wasn't anything you could find anywhere on Earth. The red eyes. It was like they had a fire in them, way down inside.'

'I believe you,' Eve assured her. Luke nodded.

It was confirmed. They had another demon in their town.

'Friday night. Woo-hoo!' Eve muttered to herself as she got in the car next to her mom. She and Luke and probably Jess – she was still working on getting a yes from her parents – had decided to meet up for more research and woo-woo practice. Luke had been really psyched about the diary entry written by Eve's great-great-great-grandmother. He was eager to find out what else Eve could do with her powers.

Usually Eve and Jess and the rest of the girls did what they called 'the prowl' on Friday nights, just the whole group of them going out together, doing anything that was fun. But what with Ms Taylor's body being discovered yesterday and Kyle's death, Deepdene was mostly shut down. People were doing only what was necessary – popping to the grocery store, the drugstore, places like that. Hardly anyone was going out to eat or to the movies or do anything else social. They were too shaken up, too afraid to leave their homes.

'You look nice,' her mom said. She raised one eyebrow. 'So nice I'm starting to worry about the next AmEx bill.'

'I didn't go too crazy this month,' Eve reassured her. She ran her fingers over the delicate heather-grey wool of her new sweater. She hadn't been able to resist it when she'd spotted it while window-shopping on Main Street. The way it criss-crossed in front made the fabric drape perfectly.

'Just as long as you don't spend so much time shopping that you let your grades slip. You've got to keep your focus on—'

'Getting the grades to get into college,' Eve finished with a little sigh. Since she'd started high school a few months ago, Eve and her mom had had this conversation many times. She flipped on the radio, hoping her mom would take the hint that they didn't need to have the college talk again. It seemed to work. Her mother started humming along instead of lecturing.

Eve's lips twitched as she wondered how her mom would react if Eve told her it wasn't the shopping that was taking up her studying time. It was the demons.

This demon is going to be so much easier to deal with than Mal was, Eve thought. It was at least part dog, for starters. It wouldn't be as clever and devious, would it? Eve flexed her fingers. Whatever the doggie brought, she felt ready to face it. She was more in control of her powers than she'd been the last time she'd had to kill a demon.

Don't get too cocky, she warned herself. *You're still talking demon. And at least two people are already dead.*

Her stomach soured. People were already dead. She knew Jess and Luke would want to be with her for the fight, but they didn't have her power. She couldn't imagine her world without Jess. Jess had been there for almost every important moment of Eve's entire life, and vice versa.

And Luke . . . They hadn't been friends all that long

at all, but she didn't even want to think about the aching hole that would be left inside her if anything happened to him. *Don't think about it then*, she told herself. *Think about something good.*

The first thing that popped into Eve's head was Luke again. But this time, Luke and luuurve. Had Jess been right about him? Did he have the hots for Eve?

When she thought about it, it did seem as if lately Luke had been looking at her a little more. But maybe that was just because the Deepdene Witch was going to have to jump into action again, and he was worried about her.

He'd held her in his arms outside the office yesterday. But that hadn't been about Eve. Not really. It was about giving comfort to someone who was scared and shocked. And it had weirded them both out a little.

Still, remembering the moment sent a rush of warmth through Eve's body. She'd wanted to hold on to him for ever. Was that just because of being scared and shocked? *You're not trying to decide if you like him; you're trying to decide if he likes you*, she told herself. Within about a week of meeting Luke, Eve had known she was never going to *like* like him. He was a player, and falling for a player could only lead to a broken heart.

But if he luuurves you, he wouldn't be a player any more, a little voice whispered in her head, a little voice that sounded annoyingly like Jess in know-it-all mode.

'Players don't fall in love,' Eve said aloud.

'What?' her mother asked.

'Nothing,' Eve answered. She was sure her mother would think luuurve would be a major distraction from doing everything that needed to be done to get into a good college.

They turned onto Margery Lane, and a few moments later her mother pulled to a stop in front of the rectory. 'Have fun,' she said.

'I will.' Eve climbed out of the car and started for the church next door. They'd decided to meet there. With a demon on the loose, they thought the extra protection of the church's gargoyles was a good idea.

But as she walked towards the safety of the church, a sense of *wrongness* filled Eve. She had the itchy feeling that someone was watching her. She didn't hear any footsteps, but still she could have sworn someone – or something – was following her.

She took a quick glance over her shoulder and didn't see anything but shadows in the growing darkness. *It's the dark that's making you nervous*, she told herself. *And the shadows.* Malphas's demons had sometimes taken on the form of shadows.

You're almost there, she thought. She was halfway across the church courtyard now. She tried to keep thinking about Luke. That had been a good distraction from bad thoughts before.

He'd known that she would want hot chocolate when they went to Java yesterday. That meant he'd noticed things about her. Noticing usually indicated some level of like. But Luke was the kind of player who liked all the girls he flirted with. He wasn't just trying to get something over on them.

The disturbing feeling of being followed hadn't disappeared when she started thinking about Luke again. Actually it was a little stronger. *No one's there*, Eve told herself. She wanted to check again, but didn't. That would be giving in to her nerves.

Almost as soon as she had that thought, she heard a rush of footsteps coming towards her. Fast. Before she could yell or turn round something clamped over her mouth and an arm pressed against her throat. She could take only the shallowest of breaths.

The platforms of her boots skidded across the paving stones as Eve was pulled across the courtyard. She gave a jerk, trying to break free. The grip on her didn't loosen at all. God, it was strong! An image flashed through Eve's brain – her body, covered in claw marks and bites, all her blood drained.

Not gonna happen. She slammed her elbow back, using every particle of strength she had. Her attacker gave a grunt. The arm around her throat let up a little. Eve twisted her head and managed to bite one of the fingers covering her mouth, tasting salty blood. Fingers, so it wasn't the dog that had been at the school. Unless it could change forms. Mal and the others had been able to.

The creature hissed with rage as Eve managed to slide down its body and out of its grasp. She spun round to face the demon – arms outstretched in front of her.

Trench stood a few feet away, his body crouched in a fighting stance. Trench? The reporter? Was he the demon? He was always lurking around somewhere – at the funeral, at Java, at school. Why hadn't she put it all together?

The man growled and slowly advanced on her. Eve gasped, fear filling her mind.

But she couldn't afford to be afraid.

She shoved all her thoughts away, squeezed her eyes shut and focused on her power. As she concentrated it quickly grew bright, brighter than the moon. When Eve felt it fill her body – toes to head to hands – she let out a scream of fear and anger and shot out two bolts.

She opened her eyes in time to see Trench fall to the ground. Eve backed away a step. Trench's body was spasming, his coat smouldering. He managed to turn his head towards Eve. His eyes glistened with hatred and rage. Well, Eve had plenty of rage too. Demons! Why couldn't they just go limp and *die*?

She thrust out her hands again, aiming at Trench. Lightning edged in flames flew from her fingertips, arced through the air and struck him. He let out a howl as his coat caught fire. *Deserved it*, Eve thought wildly. *That thing was ugly*.

He began rolling over and over to put the fire out. The second blast hadn't killed him. Far from it. As soon as the fire was out, Trench leaped to his feet. He reached behind him and whipped out a wicked-looking sword. He raised it over his head.

Before he could make another move, Eve let her power fly, her hair storming around her face, each strand electric. Trench jerked the sword towards the orange-tipped lightning bolts hurtling towards him. He laughed as the bolts hit the steel of the sword and exploded into a shower of harmless sparks.

Eve jerked her hands down, aiming at Trench's legs, and blasted again. Faster than she would have thought possible, Trench dropped to the ground and rolled over and onto his knees, slashing the sword out in time to intercept her lightning bolts and repel them.

All right. See what you can do with this, she thought as he gracefully regained his feet. This time as she threw her power out she moved her hands from side to side, sending bolts at Trench from many directions almost simultaneously.

One glanced off his shoulder, causing him to release an agonized groan. But the rest he intercepted, his body bending forward, then arcing back, as he swung his sword quickly enough to meet each bolt. The metal turned a glowing red around the edges.

Could she melt it? Was that possible? *Remember Annabelle. Anything's possible*, she told herself.

Maybe. Maybe when she was fully juiced. But the level of power in the reservoir had gone down. Eve took a breath, gathered all that remained. This time she didn't try to hit Trench's body. This time she aimed at the sword. The bolts crackled and spat as they hit the steel – then they shattered into sparks.

She was not giving up. Eve kept shoving her power out, until her fingertips were able to release only a few brief flickers, so weak they disintegrated before they reached Trench. Her power was gone. She couldn't fight him any more.

There was only one thing to do. Eve ran. The church was so close. If she could reach it . . . She pumped her legs harder. Why was she wearing fashion boots and not boot boots? She could hear Trench coming after her, and clearly he had sensible footwear. He crashed into Eve, slamming her up against the big church door. Pain coursed through every bone. She gave a choked cough as the air left her lungs.

Trench raised the sword high over his head. Eve had nothing left. She tried to draw up enough power to strike him, but all she got was a weak prickling sensation in her fingers.

The sword came down. Eve shrieked.

And somehow she was falling, falling before the blade could touch her. When she landed she saw Luke standing over her. He'd opened the church door she'd been leaning against just in time to save her. Eve scrambled deeper into the church on her hands and knees.

'Get away from her!' Luke ordered, moving between Eve and Trench.

'Out of my way, boy!' Trench shouted. 'I plan to run this demon through!'

Chapter Eight

Luke lunged at the man and grabbed one of his arms, then yanked as hard as he could. The guy barely even flinched. He was stronger than he looked. But Luke had to get that sword before he managed to kill Eve.

'She's not a demon, you idiot!' Luke shouted.

'You've let her beautiful exterior fool you!' the reporter yelled back. 'She's evil made flesh.'

His words made no sense – this whole situation made no sense – but Luke tried to follow them. This guy clearly wasn't a regular reporter, and he seemed to think Eve was a demon. Why would he even believe demons actually existed? Who was he really? It didn't matter.

'Consecrated ground!' Luke burst out. 'We're in the church. Look at all these gargoyles! How can she stand to be here if she's a demon?'

A flicker of doubt crossed Trench's face, and he hesitated. Luke took advantage of the moment. He released the man's arm, grabbed Eve, helped her to her feet and pulled her further inside. 'Look!' he shouted. '*In* the church. *In*.'

Trench lowered his sword, but he didn't put it away. 'Powerful. I've never seen a demon with this kind of resistance.' He stared first at Eve, then around the church. 'But I have powers of my own. I am drawn to demons, pulled towards them whenever they are close to me. I was led to her, and I am going to stop the massacre she has begun.'

Eve let out a gasp. 'I haven't killed anyone.'

Luke addressed Trench. 'You're wrong! What's it going to take to convince you?' he demanded. An answer flashed into his head. He grabbed Eve's hand and pulled her over to the baptismal font in the antechamber. Then he scooped some holy water up in his hands and turned and dumped it over her head.

'Hey!' Eve protested, water running down her face.

'No burns, see? Holy water, and no burns. How can she be a demon?'

Trench's brows drew together in confusion. Before he could speak, Jess came running through the door. She stopped short when she saw them at the font.

'Oh my God, what did you do to Evie's hair?' she cried. Luke let out a burst of inappropriate, near-hysterical laughter. Jess glared at him, then looked over at Trench, who still held his sword at his side. 'What exactly is going on here?'

Only Jess would ask those questions in that order, Luke thought.

Eve raced to her friend and pulled her away from Trench. 'That's what *I* want to know. Who are you and why are you here and – oh, yeah – why did you just try to kill me?'

'Who walks around with a sword?' Luke added.

Trench didn't answer Jess. He didn't even look at her. His eyes were locked on Eve. 'Don't move!' he commanded. Then he strode to the other side of the church, pulling his cell from his pocket as he went. Luke heard him begin to speak in a low, frantic tone.

Luke sighed. 'I guess it's pointless to tell that psycho that he's not allowed to use his cell in the church.' He'd hoped to lighten the mood a little, but Eve and Jess didn't laugh.

Eve's eyes glinted with fury as she used her fingers to comb her sodden hair away from her face. 'He tells *me* not to move! As if I'm going to take orders from him. What are we going to do with him? He's in the church, so he's clearly not a demon either. Although he was acting exactly like one.' She turned to Luke. 'Thanks for the save, by the way. But did you really have to destroy my hair to do it?'

'Curly hair is very difficult to manage when wet,' Jess added.

'Looks pretty much the same as always to me,' Luke joked. He tucked one of her curls behind her ear, his knuckles brushing across her cheek. As he touched her, it felt as if an electric current were running from her body into his, speeding up his heartbeat. What was that about? He'd never gotten that kind of sensation from barely touching a girl. Maybe it was her power, jumping into him? Or—

Trench stomped back over to them, yanking Luke away from his thoughts.

'Mister, you'd better explain yourself. Start with the sword,' Jess ordered, hands planted on her hips, her blue eyes flashing.

'The sword, and exactly why you were using it to try to kill Eve,' Luke added.

'Kill? You were trying to kill Eve?' Jess's voice got higher with every word.

'I'm OK,' Eve told her best friend. 'Really.'

'That's not the point,' Luke told her. 'I mean, of

course it's the most important thing, but I want this guy to start giving us some answers.'

'A lot of answers,' Eve added, hands on hips.

Trench sighed. 'I suppose I do owe you an explanation.'

'Damn right you do,' Luke muttered.

'My name is Willem Payne. I belong to an . . . well, an association of sorts: *Malleus Diabolus.* We call it the Order. We hunt demons – and we kill them. It is the reason the Order exists, and any of our members would lay down their life in the pursuit of these evil creatures.'

'So you're in a demon-hunting club?' Jess asked, sceptical.

'The Order was formed thousands of years ago. We have kept the darkness at bay for millennia,' Payne retorted, sounding a little offended. Eve shot Luke a *yeah-right* look. He nodded back. Clearly this Order of Payne's hadn't kept all the 'darkness at bay'. Malphas, Prince of Hell, for example. He'd walked right into Deepdene High.

'The death of Kyle Rakoff came to our attention,' Payne continued. 'The manner of his murder led us to suspect that he was the victim of a demon attack. I was selected to come to Deepdene to investigate and, if necessary, kill the demon responsible. It wasn't hard to blend in. Everyone assumed I was one of the reporters.'

'There's a whole group somewhere that fights demons?' Eve asked. She sounded as if she was having a hard time wrapping her head around the concept. Luke was too. But the idea that there were people out there who knew about demons, who knew what they were really up against here – that was a relief. He, Eve and Jess had been practically dealing with the whole demon thing blindfold, with only scraps of information, like the holy-water thing.

'Fine. Good. I can get behind demon killing. I'm all for it. And you want to help hunt down the demon that killed Kyle – great,' Luke told him. 'But why did you go after Eve? What made you think she was a demon?'

Jess gave an outraged yelp. 'You thought Eve was a demon?'

'Members of the Order have the ability to sense demons. In fact, this talent is what the Order is based on. Tonight I felt a pull towards the girl. It's the first time I've been close enough,' Payne answered. 'I still can hardly believe the girl is human.'

'The girl is standing right here, you know?' Eve snapped.

Payne dipped his head towards Eve. 'I apologize for attacking you. My demon sense has never led me in the wrong direction before. I'm still struggling to understand what happened.'

'What happened is that you almost turned me into a shish kebab with that sword of yours!' Eve exclaimed.

'What's the deal with the sword anyway?' Luke asked. Now that he had the chance to really look at it, he saw that the blade was etched with archaic symbols and the handle had protrusions shaped like demon faces.

'It takes a sacred weapon to kill a demon. This was blessed by one of the holy of holies. It's one of only thirteen, although three have recently been destroyed. As far as the Order knows, only these swords have the power to destroy a demon.' He looked at Eve. 'Although that perhaps is untrue. What I saw you do tonight, the fire from your hands, is that a weapon against the dark ones?'

'Too right,' Jess told him. 'You thought she was a demon, but Eve is a demon killer. She's a hero!'

Luke smiled. He loved Jess.

'There are so many things I need to ask you. How your powers work . . . your experiences with demons . . .' Payne told Eve. 'But first I need to understand why I was led to you. I just reported what happened to the leaders of my group. There's nothing in our long history to account for why my demon sense would malfunction this way.'

Eve didn't answer him. Luke got it. He wasn't sure if they should trust Payne either, although he definitely wanted access to any information Payne had.

Payne looked at Eve. 'I've told you the truth. I've apologized, and it was sincere. I'm deeply ashamed that I came so close to murdering a human,' he said.

'OK. I guess,' Eve replied, frowning.

'I understand your reluctance to confide in me. But there is still a demon to be dealt with in your town, and before I can find and destroy it I need to understand why I was pulled to *you.* It may be that only by following you can I find the true demon.' Payne finally sheathed his sword, and then he took a step closer to Eve. 'I need your help, or the demon will take the life of another innocent.'

Eve crossed her arms and kept her eyes on Payne as he read a few of the pages that they had found in the church. Luke had brought them over from the rectory. She wasn't sure they should have given Payne anything. Who knew who he really was? Who knew if any ancient order of demon hunters even existed? Still, at least two people were dead, and if there was even a possibility that Payne could help them figure out how to kill the demon responsible, they had to work with him.

Jess sidled up to Eve. 'You're wearing your gorgeous new sweater. And those tights that make your legs look like they keep on going for ever,' she whispered.

'So?' Eve whispered back, keeping her gaze on Payne.

'So I'm just wondering if there was a Luke factor in the decision to look so hot. That's not what you were wearing at school today,' Jess said, speaking directly into Eve's ear.

'What? No!' Eve forgot to whisper, and Luke and Payne both stared at her. She waved her hands. 'Never mind. Nothing.'

Jess reached over and pulled one shoulder of Eve's sweater down a tiny bit. Then she gave a satisfied smile.

Eve pulled the sweater back up. But she knew Jess had already seen what she wanted to see: the strap of Eve's makes-my-on-the-small-side-breasts-look-superb bra. Which she'd worn because . . . because it was on the top of the pile in her dresser. Although she supposed she could have worn the same bra she'd worn to school that day.

To be honest, she also supposed Jess could be exactly right about why she'd worn this outfit. It might not have anything to do with what was on top of the pile.

Why am I even thinking about this now? she asked herself. *A guy who tried to kill me less than an hour ago is sitting right over there!* Eve returned her attention to him. A moment later he looked up.

'This raises many questions,' Payne said. The papers they'd let him read talked about the Deepdene Witch and her ability to kill demons with fire from her hands. 'I need to know more.'

Says the guy who just tried to stab me with a sword, Eve thought. Should she trust this man? She glanced over at Luke for a second opinion. He gave a slight nod.

'I'm a descendant of the Deepdene Witch,' Eve told Payne. 'I had no idea that was the deal until just a few months ago, when my "powers", I guess you'd call them, started showing up.'

'For months Eve was blowing out light bulbs and TVs and computers. Doors would slam without anyone touching them when she was around,' Jess jumped in. 'We thought maybe she had a poltergeist.'

'Really?' Luke asked, surprised.

'It fitted,' Eve replied. 'Until I started shooting lightning out of my fingers. That felt like me, like something I was doing, not like something some crazy spirit was doing to me.'

'I experienced the lightning for myself,' Payne said. 'Was tonight typical?'

'I've never used my powers to attack a human before. Clearly they don't work the same way. Which is lucky for you, or you'd be dead,' Eve admitted. 'When I shot the bolts at a demon, the demon went up in smoke. With the master demon it took a bunch of blasts, but eventually I got rid of him.'

'That's probably why you get the demon vibe from Eve!' Jess cried. 'Because she zapped Mal. She probably got Mal-ness all over her.'

'Nice image. Thanks for that,' Eve said, a shudder of revulsion rippling through her.

Jess gave Eve's shoulder a rub. 'Sorry.'

Payne stood up from his pew and rejoined the group. 'Who is Mal?'

'Malphas is a demon who shows up in Deepdene every hundred years,' Luke told him.

'He was awful. He kissed people to suck out their souls,' Jess added. 'All the people who lost their souls went crazy.'

'Their souls went back to them when Eve blasted Mal away,' Luke said. 'Right before he . . . we don't really know if he died or if he's just gone for another century – anyway, right before Eve turned him to smoke, he vomited up globs of light. It seemed like those were all the souls he'd stolen. They flew off to where they belonged.'

Eve was glad her friends were telling most of the story. It was still hard for her to remember that night, to think about how drawn she had been to Mal, how close she had come to giving in to him, to kissing him and forgetting about everything else, her town, her family, her friends . . . her soul.

She pulled in a deep breath and forced herself to contribute. 'He said that he commanded forty legions of demons. He said he was the Prince of Hell and he was going to rule the world.'

Payne's eyebrows shot up. 'I find it difficult to believe a demon of that power was on Earth and my order didn't know about it. And we knew nothing of a Deepdene Witch.' He shook his head. 'I thought . . . We thought we knew everything about demons. Now it seems there is much more to learn.'

'Lots more. You didn't know there was another way to kill a demon either,' Jess pointed out. 'You thought only one of your swords would work. But Eve can do it too, with just her hands. I'm right that that's why she has the demon stink, aren't I?'

'All the members of the Order have killed demons. I've never felt the pull of a demon from them, never sensed evil,' Payne answered.

'But you don't kill demons the same way,' Luke said. 'Maybe that's why.'

Payne shrugged. 'We will have to discuss it when I return to the Order,' he answered. 'Now, tell me this, where did Malphas come from?'

'Ohio, I think,' Jess offered. Eve, Luke and Payne all stared at her. 'Oh, duh! That wasn't really true. That's just what Mal told people as his cover story. You know, I never realized that before!'

'I meant what portal.'

Eve could tell Payne was struggling to control his impatience, but she had no idea what he was talking about. 'I don't know anything about portals,' she said. 'There was nothing about them in the papers our old minster hid, at least not in the parts Luke's translated so far.'

Payne gave a sigh of frustration. 'How to explain it? Are any of you familiar with the television show *Buffy the Vampire Slayer*?' he asked.

Now they all stared at him, and Eve couldn't help laughing. This scruffy man with a huge sword, who hunted demons and sensed evil . . . he watched TV?

'Sure. We love *Buffy*,' Jess said. 'When we were in sixth grade it was on every day after school, and we were in front of the TV!'

'I've seen it a few times,' Luke agreed.

'Well, it got almost everything wrong,' Payne told them, 'but what the show called the "hellmouth" is a portal, a place where demons can pass from their world into this one. There are many such places, mystical centres where the boundary between worlds is thin. Did Malphas seem to have a home base?'

'The Razor place,' Eve said, just as Luke said, 'The old Medway mansion.'

'Which are the same house,' Jess explained. 'What you call it usually depends on how old you are. But it was the Medway mansion first.'

'Take me there. It's the most likely location of the

portal,' Payne instructed them. 'This is something I have to investigate.'

'We will. But not tonight,' Eve said quickly, before either of her friends had a chance to reply. 'I'm . . . I'm still really shaken up. I did almost get killed.' She gave Payne a pointed look. 'I need to wait until tomorrow, when it's light and I'm not so freaked.'

'Let's meet at Java Nation in the morning,' Luke suggested. 'Then we'll all walk over there together.'

'Nine.' The way Payne said it, it wasn't a question.

'Nine,' Eve agreed.

Payne left the church without another word, shutting the door behind him with a sharp click.

'Wow.' Jess shook her head. 'That was – wow.'

'Let's give him a few minutes so he won't see us,' Eve said.

'See us what?' Luke shoved his fingers through his hair.

'See us go to the Razor place. What else?' Eve asked.

'But you said you were freaked and you didn't want to go over there when it's dark,' Jess said, confused.

'True and true. But I also want to find the portal when the psycho – possible psycho, at least – with the sword isn't around,' Eve explained. 'I don't trust him. Obviously. So are you coming or not?' she asked, already knowing the answer. They were going with her.

'Like we'd let you go by yourself,' Jess said.

'Let's move it out.' Luke started for the door. 'We have a portal to find – a portal that leads to hell!'

Chapter Nine

'This place truly feels haunted now,' Eve said when they reached the Medway mansion, or what was left of it. As she stood on the sidewalk looking at it she could almost see Mal in front of her. She could picture all the renovations he'd made to the place, restoring the sunken tennis courts, the formal gardens and every detail of the huge Georgian house. When she'd smoked him, the mansion had immediately begun to crumble, reverting to the ruin it had been, the gardens returning to wildness. Had all the work been nothing but illusion?

'Do you think the portal could be the reason there've always been ghost stories about the mansion?' Jess asked.

'Maybe,' Eve answered. The ghost stories had gotten wilder since the destruction of the mansion. Some people claimed ghosts were responsible.

Some thought Mal and his family had done the damage themselves. Some even blamed a freak earthquake, one that affected only that stretch of land. 'We have to find a way to close the portal fast, before anyone else gets hurt.'

'Fill me in on what people say about the mansion,' Luke said. 'I don't know all the town stories yet.'

'Nobody has ever lived in the house for much more than a year,' Jess said.

'This is where Razor killed himself,' Eve added.

'Razor? As in *Empty Tables*?' Luke tossed out the name of the rock star's most famous CD.

'Yeah, he was the last person to live there before Mal. The place completely fell apart after he died. That's when talk of the house being haunted was really big, at least according to Megan's mom – she's the realtor,' Jess said. 'All the other people who took the house before Razor just left, which was weird enough. The software genius who owned the place just before Razor didn't even bother to pack. Then with a suicide . . .'

'No one wanted to move in,' Eve finished for her. 'Even though it's impossible to find places for sale in the Hamptons.'

'I guess it would be hard for even a brilliant

real-estate agent to spin. Is there any positive way to say "comes with its own portal to hell"?' Luke asked.

Eve looked at the ruins for a moment more. 'Let's go,' she finally said. She led the way up the overgrown path leading to the mansion.

'Um, does anyone know what a hell portal actually looks like?' Jess asked.

'It was in the basement of the school on *Buffy*. You couldn't really see it though, right?' Luke asked.

Eve nodded. 'I guess we'll just have to figure it out as we go. Maybe it will smell like wood-smoke the way the demons do.' She walked over to the wide stone steps that led up to the front door. *Used to lead*, she corrected herself. Now they led nowhere, and were surrounded by rubble. She ran her finger over the top step. It was cool to the touch, but that was all, and that was completely ordinary.

She took out her keychain and clicked on the little LED light. Shining the thin bright beam over the wreckage, Eve thought she spotted one of the orbed feet of the chaise longue where she and Mal had sat together the night he made her dinner, the night she'd destroyed him. She swung the light to the left and saw sparkling shards of glass from the doors that had opened onto the garden. Those doors had given a beautiful view of the rose bushes and the dovecote.

'The dovecote!' Eve exclaimed. 'Maybe that's where the portal is. I remember how it looked so cute from the outside the first time I saw it, like a big stone beehive. But then there weren't doves nesting in the little cubbies inside; there were crows.' She turned to Luke. 'And part of what you translated said that crows were attracted to the master demon. Maybe they'd be attracted to the portal too, since that's where the demon comes from. Maybe the dovecote was over the portal.'

'It's as good a place to start as any.' Luke, Jess and Eve walked to the heap of stones that once formed the dovecote. Eve was glad they were all together. She really would rather do this during the day. But if there was something to find here, she wanted advance knowledge. She wanted to keep ahead of Payne in every way until she decided whether or not she could trust him.

'So if we find the portal, do we tell Trenchie?' Jess asked.

'I don't know,' Eve answered. 'I know he said he was a good guy—'

'But he tried to kill you,' Luke interrupted. 'Maybe it's because his demon sense told him to. Maybe not. Maybe there's no such thing as a demon sense. Maybe there's no such thing as that order he was talking about. Maybe he's working *with* the demons and that's why he tried to kill Eve.'

'That's way too many maybes,' Jess said.

'I don't want to tell Payne anything yet. We really don't know anything about him,' Eve said.

'Your call,' Luke told her. 'And I agree with you. I'd love to have help going after this demon, but we need proof that Payne is on our side.'

They returned to their search. Eve circled the jumble of stones slowly, trying to *feel* as much as look. There wasn't much to look at. Besides the stones, there were a few black feathers and some splotches of bird poop. She didn't feel anything. No tingle in her fingers, nothing to hint that there was something beyond what she saw with her eyes. Maybe that wasn't one of her powers.

'Do you think if we step in the wrong place we'll just go through?' Jess asked. 'I'm asking because I don't think I'm dressed for hell.'

Eve laughed. Somehow Jess could always make her laugh. 'What does dressed for hell look like?'

'I have to think about it. But definitely higher heels,' Jess answered. 'Probably a really deep-red lipstick. Although maybe that's a cliché.'

Luke would usually come up with some type of snarkasm at this point, but he didn't say anything. Eve looked over at him and saw that he was staring at a pointed arch of smooth, pale grey stone amidst the ruins. It looked much older than the Georgian-style ruins that surrounded it, and it was the only structure that was intact. 'You think?' Eve asked.

'I saw a sketch of an arch really similar to that one in the papers from the church,' Luke answered. 'Same Gothic style. Those weird markings carved into it look the same too. What I was reading said they were part of an ancient text that no one has ever been able to decipher.'

Eve squinted at the markings, then moved closer and shone her LED light on them. They were just words, not weird markings at all. She looked over her shoulder at Luke. 'You decided this was a good time to mess with me?'

Luke stretched his arms out wide. 'What?'

'The ancient text on our arch here is English,' she informed him. As if he hadn't realized that.

Luke and Jess exchanged a puzzled look. 'Like really *Old* English?' Jess asked.

'You too?' Eve said. She turned away from them and climbed over the wreckage of the house to get closer to the arch. She shone the light on the words again. 'On the hundred-year mark, thy hand or thy blood must the portal open.'

Jess and Luke stepped up beside her. 'That's what you see?' Jess asked, her voice trembling a little.

'Yes.' Eve studied her friend's face. She looked scared. This wasn't some joke. 'Oh. You two don't, do you? You really don't.'

'I see . . . I don't know what they are. Pictures or hieroglyphs or something,' Jess said.

Luke nodded agreement.

Eve didn't know what to say. She'd gotten used to having lightning in her hands, but this weirdness was new.

Jess reached out and took Eve's hand. 'I'm so glad we came without Payne,' Eve said. 'He'd be pulling out his sword right now. This would convince him I'm a demon.'

'Or maybe he'd just take it as more proof that you're the Deepdene Witch,' Luke told her. 'That's the scenario that makes sense to me.' He began grabbing stones and pieces of wood and tossing them aside, clearing the area in front of the arch. No more words were revealed. Luke tapped the arch. 'Feels normal. But what do I know? Should I try stepping through?'

'No!' Eve and Jess exclaimed together.

'We need a lot more information – and, according to Jess, some new shoes and lipstick – before we do that,' Eve said.

'I thought this was OK for hell casual.' Luke gestured to his jeans, T-shirt and distressed leather jacket.

'Probably is. But that's no reason to go through,' Eve told him firmly. She grabbed him by the back of the jacket and towed him a few steps away from the arch.

'I bet this is why the police and the search teams haven't found anything in the woods,' Luke said. 'I bet the demon comes through here, kills someone and then goes back through the portal until it's time for the next attack.'

'You know what?' Eve asked. 'I'm thinking we should continue this conversation somewhere not so close to the demon's door. Like back at the church.' She managed a small smile. 'Since we can all tolerate consecrated ground.'

'Good idea,' Luke said.

They picked their way back over the rubble.

'Uh-oh,' Eve said as they started down the sidewalk. Payne was striding towards them.

'Nine o'clock got here so fast,' Jess said brightly when he stopped in front of them.

A smile twitched at the corner of Payne's lips. 'Good morning to you.'

So he had a sense of humour. Hmm. That didn't mean he was trustworthy, but it made Eve start to like him. A little. For a person who had tried to murder her.

'I guess pretty much anyone in town could tell you how to get to the Razor place,' Luke commented.

'Yes,' Payne answered. 'And the situation is too serious for me to wait until morning. By then the demon could have taken another victim.'

Payne could be lying. Like Luke said, he could be on the side of the demons. But Eve thought she'd heard something in his voice, some of the worry she felt about not being able to protect the people of Deepdene even with her powers.

'We . . . yeah. We think the situation is pretty bad too,' Eve told him. 'We thought we'd take a look tonight.' She didn't mention the arch. She was feeling a little more ready to trust the man, but she wasn't going to tell him about the strange markings only she could read. At least not yet.

Payne locked eyes with her. 'I can hardly imagine

what it was like for you, discovering the existence of demons with no one to guide you. I had years of instruction before my first battle with a dark one. Even then I did not face it alone.'

'I'm not alone either,' Eve pointed out.

'She has us,' Jess added.

'Is the Order big? How many members?' Luke asked.

'It's much smaller than it once was. In our early days everyone believed in demons. People understood us . . . appreciated us. When someone with the ability to sense demons was discovered, they were directed to us,' Payne said. 'Now . . . believers are far fewer. Warriors with the talent and training to battle a demon are even rarer than that. I'm sure if our numbers were greater we would have been aware of you and your abilities,' he told Eve. 'One of us would have been by your side when you faced your first demon.'

Things might have been so different if she'd had more information, information this Order could perhaps have given her. She'd smelled wood-smoke the first time she met Mal, but it hadn't rung any warning bells. She'd had to figure out for herself that demons and the scent came together.

Eve's muscles tensed as she realized there was a slight scent of it in the air. 'Do you smell that? The wood-smoke. I smell it when I'm near demons,' Eve quickly explained to Payne, willing to trust him with that much information. She had so many questions she wanted to ask him.

'I don't smell anything,' Luke answered. Jess and Payne shook their heads. Was smelling demons something only Eve could do too?

'I think I smelled it in the courtyard when we were fighting too,' Eve told Payne. 'I'm just remembering. I was so focused on killing you I didn't take it in right there.'

'Is it possible you're being followed by a dark one?' Payne asked. 'Maybe that's why I was drawn towards you. Was and am, in fact.'

Eve took a step closer to Payne. 'I think it's coming from you!' she exclaimed.

'He's a demon?' Luke burst out.

'But he was in the church too,' Jess pointed out.

Eve took one more tentative step nearer to Payne. 'It's definitely you.' Payne stayed absolutely still and Eve moved right up beside him. 'It's from here,' she said, lightly touching his back.

Payne slowly and carefully took out his sword. 'From this?' He held it out to her, careful to keep the blade pointed away.

Eve leaned down and sniffed, then looked up at him. 'Yes.'

'The details of how the swords came to be aren't fully known,' Payne told her, 'but there are stories that they were tempered in pools of demon blood. Maybe that's what you're smelling. Of course, the sword has killed many demons too.'

'The smell makes me feel like I'm about to be attacked,' Eve admitted.

'That fear is not necessarily a bad thing,' he told her. 'It can be a kind of warning system. When a demon is near, it's like I'm a fish on a line.'

'Ouch,' Jess said.

'Yeah,' Eve agreed.

'But it gives me an advance warning,' Payne told them. 'It has saved my life more than once. I felt the pull only moments before a woman, a woman whose beauty had blinded me to her true nature, transformed into the demon Apep, a huge snake with a head of flint that was impervious to my sword.'

He was taken in by a demon who looked like a hot woman. Maybe he would understand how part of me wanted to kiss Mal, even when I knew what he was, Eve thought. Luke and Jess were the best, absolutely the best. But there were some things about demons they'd probably never be able to really get in a gut way, the way Payne said he did.

'Was that the worst demon you've had to face down?' Luke asked.

Payne ran his finger down a long scar that ran along the side of his throat and disappeared under the collar of his coat. His hideous trench coat now looked even worse, thanks to the scorch marks from Eve's lightning bolts. *It's actually almost like a knight's armour*, she thought.

'No. Not the worst. Not nearly the worst,' Payne answered. 'But each demon I have faced has made me stronger. Even the one that gave me this.' He touched the scar again. 'That was the demon Ronove. He considered it his duty to take the souls of the old. He came for my grandmother.'

Eve's chest tightened.

'I was the veteran of many battles, yet—'

A long, high scream interrupted Payne. The scream was followed by a dog baying. Both sounds came from the direction of the woods on the other side of Medway Lane.

'You stay here, all of you,' Payne ordered. 'Please,' he added, before he turned and raced for the woods.

'Should we go after him?' Eve asked.

Luke hesitated. 'It sounded like he could take care of himself.'

'Especially with that sword,' Jess added.

'But you saw the scar. It's not like he can't be hurt. Or killed,' Eve said. The little hairs on the back of her neck stood up as a second scream ripped though the air.

'That's Vic!' Jess shouted. 'We're going!' She spun round and took off, running into the woods.

'This is crazy! How could she know it's Vic from those screams?' Luke asked as he and Eve raced after Jess.

'They're both on the cheerleading squad. They're always screaming and squealing together,' Eve said. 'The sound Victoria made when she got promoted to head cheerleader? It was at least as loud as what we just heard.' She lengthened her stride. 'Jess, would you please wait?' she yelled.

Jess didn't slow down. Not until she reached a clearing not far into the woods. Then she slammed to a stop so fast that Eve almost ran into her. 'Oh, God, Evie,' Jess cried.

Eve followed Jess's transfixed gaze and saw Victoria running across the clearing. A huge dog was chasing her, and Payne wasn't far behind it.

The demon. There was something wrong about its gait. When Eve realized why the creature was moving in such an unnatural way it felt like a punch to the solar plexus. It had huge claws, blade-sharp claws shaped like scythes, on all four feet.

'Vic, over here!' Luke shouted.

Victoria veered towards his voice, and the demon turned after her. Eve saw that the claws weren't the only atrocity. Like Jess had said, the demon had a face that was almost human, but warped, with a nose that was nearly non-existent. Against the sides of its head were the pointed ears of a bat. Its small eyes glowed red and held an intelligence that took Eve's breath away. It grinned, revealing insanely long, sharp teeth of a rotted-looking dingy yellow. It was enjoying itself.

The creature brayed again, white foam flying from its lips, then it stopped and tilted its head back, sniffing. *Did it just realize we're here?* Eve wondered as Payne slowly circled in front of the demon dog.

Victoria kept running towards them. 'Come on, Vic!' Jess yelled.

Eve could hear Victoria's harsh breaths. She was going to reach them. She was halfway there. The demon dog hadn't moved. Could it recognize the power in Eve? Was it afraid? It had stopped before Payne took his position in front of it.

There was a rustling in the undergrowth not far from Luke and two more of the demons burst into the clearing!

Eve felt as if her stomach had dropped to her knees. There were more of the creatures? The cheerleaders had seen only one. How many were there?

The two dogs went after Vic, blocking her way to Eve and the others. Payne and the first dog were still facing off not far behind her.

Vic froze. 'Nice dogs. Nice, nice dogs.' Her voice was shaking so violently that it was hard to make out the words. It was clear she was trying to remain motionless, but her body was trembling too, quivering with terror.

Those are not nice dogs, Eve thought, horrified. *Those are demon dogs, and they're going to rip Vic apart.*

Chapter Ten

Luke took off towards Victoria, Eve and Jess beside him. He tried to formulate some kind of plan. Maybe he could distract at least a couple of the dog-things and give Eve a chance to blast them with her power.

He scanned the ground for a rock. Anything he could use to stop the demons from attacking Vic before Payne or Eve could deal with them. He didn't see a thing. He had a vial of holy water that he'd brought from the church, thinking it could be useful, but he wasn't close enough to use it. He glanced at Eve. She was still too far to blast. They weren't going to be in time.

But Payne was faster than Luke would have thought possible. He threw his body between Victoria and the two demon dogs in front of her. The first demon was on his heels. Payne swept his sword out in front of him. 'Back!' he shouted, and his voice was like thunder.

All three demon dogs growled, but when the first one backed up a few paces the others did too.

Luke stumbled to a stop. He stuck out an arm to stop Eve and Jess as well. What was the right move here? He was afraid that if they kept running, one of the demon dogs might get spooked and launch an attack on Payne.

'Maybe if we move slowly . . .' Eve said, as if she could read his mind.

Luke took one step, and Payne spotted him.

'Stay back, you three!' he ordered.

Luke hesitated. The first demon backed up another step, angling itself towards Vic, while the other dogs continued to face Payne. The first demon dog dropped into a crouch.

'It's going to pounce,' Eve gasped.

'Payne!' Luke shouted. 'Look out! To your left!'

Too late. The muscles of the demon dog's back legs tensed, and a moment later the dog was airborne, its gruesome mouth wide open, ready to slash its knife-teeth into Vic's throat.

Again Payne moved with lightning speed, shoving Victoria backwards with one hand as he twisted his body towards the attacking demon, swinging his sword towards its neck.

Jess sprinted towards Vic, Eve and Luke on her heels. Luke heard a yelp of pain, and out of the corner of his eye he saw the first demon dog fall to the ground, blood spurting from its shoulder. Payne had managed to wound it.

Luke felt a burst of relief, but it lasted for only a second. Payne was wounded too. Blood gushed from his throat, and he pressed one hand against the deep, ragged bite mark.

Jess circled behind Payne and the dogs, so Luke followed her.

But Eve veered away from them, running straight towards one of the other demons. She skidded to a stop and threw out both hands. It didn't look as if she had much strength though. Luke couldn't really watch, since he was focusing on Jess and Vic, but at full power Eve's lightning bolts would have lit up the entire clearing. Instead there was only a brief flicker of light, a short crackling sound.

Jess reached Vic first. She hauled her to her feet and pulled her towards the woods.

That was the best thing she could do, Luke realized. 'Get her up in a tree. You too!' he shouted after them.

'Run, Luke!' Eve cried. 'I've got almost nothing left. I'll try to hold them off.'

Like he was going to leave her alone with the demons. Payne had collapsed on the ground. He might even be dead.

'Go for the one Payne stabbed!' Luke urged. It was already injured, at least, although it had regained its feet. Eve turned and shoved her hands towards the first demon dog. At the same time, Luke whipped out the bottle of holy water and flung the contents at the demon.

The demon dog yowled and skittered away. It stared at Eve, eyes narrowed, lip pulled back over its teeth. Luke had no holy water left. Eve couldn't have much juice. But the demon didn't risk attacking them.

'I don't forget,' it told Eve, and its voice was as much snarl as speech.

Eve stumbled backwards in shock, and Luke caught her to keep her from falling. He could hardly believe it had spoken at all. But its head was that of a demon, not a dog.

The injured demon turned and trotted away, limping. The other two demon dogs followed it. Eve could smell the scent of wood-smoke on them all.

'Oh my God,' Eve gasped. 'Just oh my God.'

'Payne,' Luke said.

Eve pulled in a deep breath and hurried over to the

fallen demon hunter. She and Luke both dropped to their knees beside him. He wheezed with every lungful of air he drew in but managed to raise one arm and point after the retreating demon dogs.

'Wargs,' he managed to choke out, just as Jess rejoined them.

'What?' Eve asked, leaning close to Payne. 'What did you say, Payne?'

'Wargs.' The word came out in a hissing whisper.

Eve looked at Luke. 'I didn't understand him.'

Luke hadn't either. 'Payne, one more time. I know it's important. What are you telling us?'

Payne didn't answer. Instead he reached out and nudged his sword towards Luke. Luke's chest tightened as he looked at it, but he stood and picked up the weapon. It was heavier than he had expected, and the demon faces on the hilt felt alien in his hand. Payne continued to stare at him. 'I think he wants you to put it on,' Eve said. She turned to Jess. 'Help me take off the sheath. It's strapped to his back.'

The girls unbuckled the sheath and slid it out from under Payne as gently as they could. Luke could see by Payne's face that they were hurting him, but he made no sound of pain or protest.

'Take off your jacket,' Eve said.

Luke obeyed. He felt the way he sometimes had as an acolyte for his father, lighting the candles as the service began. He felt as if he were taking part in something deeply holy.

Eve stood and assisted Luke in strapping the sheath to his back. Luke looked down at Payne as he raised the sword and slid it home.

Payne gave a small nod of approval, then let out a long, rasping breath. Luke saw the moment the life slipped away from the man, saw his eyes go blank.

The sword felt powerful pressed against his spine, like it was a part of him already. Luke hoped he could live up to the rare weapon, and to the rare man who had given it to him.

Chapter Eleven

'He's dead.' Eve stared down at Payne. The blood from the ragged bite of the demon dog had stopped gushing. His eyes had turned to big glassy marbles, all the life gone from them.

Eve knelt down beside Payne again. She'd never been this close to a dead body. She hadn't seen the demon dogs' other victims after they were killed. Seeing Payne lying there made everything so much more real.

She reached out a hand and used her palm to slide Payne's eyes closed. She could have learned so much from him. And she knew that, as a demon fighter himself, he would have understood her in a way that even Jess and Luke didn't. They could understand a lot. They'd even experienced a lot themselves. But it wasn't quite the same.

'We have to figure out a way to contact the Order.

They need to know what happened to Payne,' Eve said.

'And what's still happening here,' Luke said. 'It would be great if we could get reinforcements.'

'The first thing we have to do is call an ambulance,' Jess said.

'He doesn't need one, not any more,' Luke answered.

'And what would we say?' Eve asked. 'We can't exactly tell people that he was killed by a pack of demons. They'd send us straight to Ridgewood. I know it's the poshest mental hospital in the state, but still.'

'We can figure out something to tell them. We can't leave his body out here. What if those things come back and tear him up?' Jess hugged herself. 'We can't just leave him.'

Eve reached out and squeezed her best friend's hand. Jess looked wiped, and she knew she probably looked even worse. They were all in shock.

'I better go help Vic down,' Jess said. She turned and headed back towards the trees.

'I guess we just say we found a body that looks like it's been mauled by wild animals.' Luke pulled his jacket on, hiding Payne's sword on his back. Then he took his cell out of his jacket pocket. 'We don't have to tell them we saw it happen.'

Eve nodded. 'Do you think Victoria got a good look at the demons though? What do you think she'll say to the paramedics?'

'Doesn't matter what she says,' Luke answered. 'If she starts talking about how the dogs had hideous half-human faces, they'll just think she's losing it because she's scared. Which she probably is.'

'Yeah, you're right. Luke . . . ?' Eve hesitated.

'What?'

'Did you hear the first demon dog say something?'

'Yeah. It said, "I don't forget." But you know what? We don't either. That puppy is—'

'I just wasn't sure,' Eve interrupted him. 'I thought it might be like the markings on the arch, something only I could understand. I'm glad you heard it too.'

'I definitely did,' he said. 'Ambulance?'

'Yeah. Call,' Eve said. She gazed across the clearing, checking on Jess and Vic. Vic was almost out of the tree. As Eve watched, she jumped from a low branch to the ground and Jess wrapped her in a hug.

Eve pushed herself to her feet and turned away from Payne's body. From this angle the clearing was beautiful, the ground crunching with newly fallen leaves, surrounded by trees, with a half-moon high in the sky. Eve loved half-moons. The shape seemed happy somehow, a sideways smile. On a different night, in a Deepdene without demons, she could imagine herself sitting there staring up at the moon for dreamy hours. Maybe even with a late-night picnic. Would Luke think that was silly?

'They're on their way,' Luke said, pulling Eve away from her thoughts. Her silly thoughts. Before anyone could picnic in the woods there were demons to kill. She was the Deepdene Witch. She was responsible for the safety of her town and everyone who lived there.

'Do you think it's OK if I take Vic home?' Jess asked as she and Victoria joined them. 'She's wrecked. She doesn't need to be questioned about every detail. She needs to get herself into a tub of vanilla-cupcake bubble bath, put on a cooling eye mask and listen to "Soul Meets Body" a whole bunch of times.'

'Eve and I can handle things,' Luke replied. 'We're going to say we stumbled on the body. It's dark. We'll say we didn't see anything. There's no reason all four of us have to be here.'

'I was just going to visit Helena,' Victoria said, her voice sounding somehow mechanical. 'My mom said

I could.' She stared out into the clearing, but Eve got the feeling she wasn't really seeing anything. She was lost in the darkness in her head.

'That's all she's said since I got her out of the tree,' Jess murmured.

'Just trying to visit Helena,' Vic repeated.

'I know, sweetie. It's OK,' Jess said. She patted Vic's shoulder.

'I wanted to be there for her. She's still so upset about Kyle.' Vic was starting to sound a little more like her regular self. She turned to Jess. 'I was trying to do something good.' Tears sprang into her eyes. 'Bad things shouldn't happen when you're trying to do something good.'

'I know, I know,' Jess crooned. 'Come on. Let's get you home now.' She looped an arm around Vic's shoulders and led her away. It looked like Victoria had just learned to walk. She kept tottering, and only Jess's arm held her upright.

Eve felt like she could use some holding up too, and, as if he'd read her thoughts, Luke put an arm around her shoulders. 'Another wild Friday night in Deepdene, huh?'

'Yeah, we know how to party around here.' Eve let her head rest against Luke's shoulder. What would she do without him? Every time things got bad, there he was, ready to help.

'You're not alone in all this,' Luke said. 'Yes, you're the big cheese and all, the Deepdene Witch. You have the powers, and you can read markings no one else can, but that doesn't mean you have to deal with this whole situation by yourself. Until the demon creatures are gone, you're not going to be able to get rid of me.'

Relief and comfort flooded her. 'I don't want to,' Eve admitted. 'Without you – you and Jess – I think I truly would end up in Ridgewood. Or I'd just be dead. My power was almost gone when I zapped that demon tonight. If you hadn't thrown the holy water, who knows what would have happened?'

'We don't need to know, because I did,' Luke answered. 'I hear the paramedics.'

A few seconds later, a man and a woman in uniform burst into the dark clearing, each holding one end of a stretcher. They went directly to Payne, and the man crouched down to check for a pulse. It took a couple of tries. His fingers kept sliding in the blood on Payne's throat.

'He's gone,' he finally pronounced. 'His jugular's slashed. At least he didn't suffer as much as . . .' He broke off, seeming to remember Eve and Luke's presence. 'The police are going to want to talk to you two. They're on the way. We'll meet them at the ambulance.'

In a few well-practised moves the paramedics loaded Payne's body onto the stretcher. They carried it across the clearing, then through the woods, zig-zagging around the trees. Eve and Luke followed behind them, holding hands, their feet crunching in the fallen leaves. It felt for a minute like they were Hansel and Gretel, wandering through a dangerous and terrifying forest.

When they broke back onto the sidewalk, they saw a police cruiser parked next to the ambulance. Two cops climbed out. One of them gestured Eve and Luke over, while the other strode to the paramedics.

They dropped hands as they walked to him, and Eve's hand felt much colder than it should have without Luke's warmth. 'What the hell were you kids thinking, being in the woods? At night. After two people were killed there in the last couple of weeks,' the cop demanded.

Eve recognized him. She recognized most people in Deepdene. She'd lived there her whole life. The cop was Officer Huft, Darby Huft's dad. He'd come to the middle school once to give a talk on Halloween safety. He'd seemed a lot more friendly then.

She swallowed hard and tried to explain. 'We just . . .' Just what? Why would they have been in the woods?

'We just wanted to be alone for a while,' Luke said, moving a little closer to Eve.

Mr Huft shook his head, disgusted. 'You can't go around thinking with your . . .' He stopped. 'You're both old enough to realize the danger here. I wish I had photos of the other bodies to show you. They were covered in bites and claw marks, and there was no blood left in them. Do you get that? This isn't a TV show. It isn't some damn video game. It's real. And it's only blind luck that we aren't putting two more bodies in there.' He pointed to the ambulance.

'Yes, sir,' Eve said.

Luke nodded.

'All right. Tell me what happened. You went into the woods looking for some alone time.' Mr Huft snorted. 'And—'

'We weren't planning to go very far in. I knew there was a clearing. I thought it would be a good place to hang out,' Luke said. Mr Huft gave another snort. Eve couldn't help thinking about how Luke's explanation was sort of like her daydream of them on a picnic.

'As soon as we got to the clearing, we knew something was wrong,' she jumped in. 'In the moonlight we saw someone lying in the grass, lying really still.'

'We ran over. But when we got closer, it was clear he was dead. There was so much blood around the wound on his throat,' Luke said.

'Did either of you touch him?' Mr Huft asked.

'I closed his eyes,' Eve volunteered.

'I think I put my head on his chest,' Luke said. 'Like I said, as soon as I got a good look at him, I knew he was dead. But I guess I panicked. I got down next to him and kind of shook him a little. Then I listened to his chest to see if I could hear a heartbeat.'

Good. Luke had explained away the evidence the police might find around Payne's body. At least the signs that she and Luke were there. They'd see evidence of the demon dogs too, but they'd think the animals had left before she and Luke arrived.

'Have you ever seen the man before?' Mr Huft asked.

'Around school and outside the church at Kyle Rakoff's funeral,' Eve replied.

'We actually saw him in Java Nation once too,' Luke added. 'We figured he was one of the reporters covering the killings. Reporters were all over the place.'

Mr Huft wrote briefly in a small spiral notebook. 'Did you see anything else out there? Animal, human, anything.'

'Maybe a squirrel or something,' Eve answered. 'I wasn't really paying attention when we were walking in, and then . . .'

She leaned against the hood of the cruiser, the events of the past hour flooding back through her. She could feel again the horrified shock as the demon creature *spoke* to her, the grief over Payne's death, even the pride she felt helping Luke strap on the sheath for the sword. Her body felt boneless, her muscles watery. It was as if all her strength had surged out of her along with her power.

'It's all hitting you now,' Mr Huft said. 'You have to learn to think about things before they happen, not after.' He opened the back door of the cruiser. 'Get in. I'll need to take you to the station to get your statements, then I'll run you both home. Going to take their statements,' he called to his partner as Eve and Luke slid into the back seat.

The time it took for Mr Huft to take their statements and drive to Eve's house was much too short. It was definitely not going to go unnoticed that she was being returned home in a police cruiser, and she hadn't managed to come up with any explanation that wouldn't give her parents heart failure.

'OK if I walk her to the door?' Luke asked.

'Yeah. And while you're up there, tell her parents that you two wanted to be alone in the woods with a wild animal,' Mr Huft said.

Luke climbed out of the car and held out his hand to help Eve out. He really could be such a sweetie sometimes. Actually, lately it was most of the time.

'You want me to help you talk to your parents?' he asked when they reached the porch.

'Better if I do it alone, I think,' Eve said.

The front door swung open. 'Eve! What's going on?' her mother exclaimed.

'I'll explain everything, but Mr Huft is waiting to drive Luke home,' Eve said. She turned to Luke. 'Let's meet up at the library tomorrow to do research for that paper we have due.'

'On ancient architecture,' Luke replied, referencing the arch to show he knew what she meant.

'First thing when it opens,' Eve said.

He turned and started down the steps. Eve felt a pang, as if something inside her had snapped. Luke turned back. 'Bye, Mrs Evergold. Bye, Eve.' He waved and gave her one of his classic Luke smiles. And somehow, miraculously, it made her feel a little better.

'Call me when you want to come home,' Eve's mother instructed as she pulled into the library parking lot the next morning. 'And don't take a step outside that building until I get here.'

'Mom, it'll be the middle of the day. I can—'

'No,' her mother interrupted. 'It's bad enough that you almost got yourself killed last night—'

'I did not,' Eve protested, although it wasn't entirely true. 'I just found that guy.'

'Because you were walking around town,' her mother said. 'Which you will not do again until the police catch these vicious animals.'

Eve sighed. 'OK.' She grabbed her bag and got out of the car.

Her mother rolled down the window. 'You call me, Eve!'

'I will! I promise!' It was October, but it was warm enough that the library had the door leading to the parking lot propped open to let in some of the lovely fresh air.

Eve walked inside and instantly spotted Jess and

Luke. They'd taken the table closest to the door. 'It's almost like being outside,' Jess said, gesturing to the sun coming in. 'Well, sort of. By which I mean, not at all.'

'I don't know if I'll ever be allowed outside again,' Eve groaned. 'My mom insisted on driving me.'

Jess pointed to herself and nodded.

'My dad dropped me off too,' Luke added.

'Our Luke has been busy,' Jess told Eve. 'He found some stuff online last night, but he wouldn't tell me anything until you got here.' She gave an exaggerated pout that quickly slid into a smile.

'Only because I didn't want to have to repeat everything,' Luke said.

'Also, I waited until now to ask him if he is wearing a puka shell necklace without a trace of irony,' Jess said. 'I didn't want him to have to repeat his answer either. So?'

'People wear them in Santa Cruz – what can I say?' Luke fingered the tiny round shells strung on a rawhide cord. 'Am I a candidate for *What Not to Wear* again?'

Eve and Jess exchanged a look and smiled. Luke was such a tease that sometimes it took both of them to tease him back properly.

'No, you're good,' Eve told him. 'If someone like Dave Perry tried to pull it off – forget it. But you make it work somehow. Maybe it's your California cool.'

'I've never had girl friends – girls who are friends – to tell me this stuff before,' Luke said.

'Well, you're just lucky you met us,' Eve told him.

'I am,' Luke answered, looking directly into her eyes. Jess gave Eve a little kick under the table. If kicks could talk, that one would have said, 'I told you so.'

'Jess, how's Victoria?' Eve asked.

'Um, pretty OK. Her mom gave her a sleeping pill. I stayed with her until it kicked in, but she didn't say much,' Jess answered.

'Did she say anything about me? About the lightning bolts?' Cos if she had, that was something they'd need to deal with.

'I don't think she took her eyes off the demon dogs until I grabbed her and pulled her up a tree,' Jess replied. 'She definitely didn't mention it when I was around.'

'Good,' Luke said. 'So after I went home, and once I'd managed to convince my dad that my police cruiser ride wasn't a reason to hyperventilate, I went online. I did a search on that word Payne said right before he died – "warg". It was obviously something he believed we had to know.'

‘Is “warg” even a word? I thought I wasn’t understanding him right,’ Eve said.

‘Oh, yeah, it’s a word.’ His backpack rested next to his chair. He opened it and pulled out some pieces of paper that had been stapled together. ‘I printed out some of what I found.’ He slid the papers in front of Eve and Jess.

The top page had a line drawing of a creature that was almost identical to the demon dogs. Ears like a bat’s; thin, wickedly sharp teeth; eyes filled with malevolence. A face that was all the more horrible because it contained some human elements.

‘So I’m thinking that’s a warg.’ Revulsion filled Jess’s voice.

‘This is great. What does it say about them? Anything we can use?’ Eve asked.

‘They’re a kind of hellhound. There have been legends about them since Viking days, according to this.’ Luke tapped the pile of papers. ‘Supposedly, at least based on what I found, there have been a few recent sightings – like in the last hundred years – around cemeteries in Connecticut and Louisiana.’

‘Connecticut’s pretty close,’ Jess said.

‘Why around cemeteries?’ Eve asked. ‘Wait. Back up more. I don’t even know what a hellhound is supposed to be. Well, I guess I've seen them, but do they have powers besides the insane teeth and claws? And the talking?'

'There was a lot of contradictory information about their powers,' Luke replied. 'Some of the myths – I guess we shouldn't call them that, since we saw the things – say that if anyone looks a hellhound in the eye three times, that person will die.'

'Oh, great,' Jess mumbled.

'Their howl is supposed to put terror into people,' Luke continued.

'If those things meowed like little kitty cats, the sound would still put terror into me,' Eve admitted. She glanced around the nearby tables to see if anyone could overhear them. Nope. Everybody must still be hiding in their houses. 'What else?'

'The leader of the hellhound pack has more powers than the other ones. It's the only one that can speak,' Luke said. 'And back to the cemetery thing – hellhounds are supposed to be gatekeepers. They guard boundaries, and a cemetery is a sort of boundary – between the living and the dead. One site said they guard portals.'

'Fantastic,' Jess said. 'Our town has been invaded by the devil's watchdogs.'

‘Did it say anything else about portals?’ Eve asked.

‘Nope,’ Luke answered. ‘And that’s all I got. I can keep researching them. I checked the library computer. There are a bunch of books on myths and legends, but I didn’t have time to pull any of them out yet.’

Jess took out her cherry-coloured Mac. She’d gotten it after Eve shorted out her old one. Electrical stuff had gone crazy around Eve in the stretch of time when her powers were beginning to come out. ‘How about if I search for dog attacks near cemeteries?’ she asked.

‘Great idea,’ Luke told her.

Jess winked at him. ‘I have many talents.’

‘Yeah, you should see the lanyard she made our first year at camp,’ Eve teased. ‘She won the prize because it was the longest out of everybody’s. And there are many uses for a lanyard twice the length of your body.’

‘What on earth is a lanyard?’ Luke asked.

‘Remember, Luke hasn’t had all the privileges we have,’ Eve teased. ‘He’s probably never been to camp,’ she said to Jess.

‘No camp for me. Except vacation Bible school at Dad’s church,’ Luke told them.

'A lanyard is just a really long rope-bracelet-necklace thingy,' Eve told him. 'You'd like it, Puka Shell Necklace Man.'

Luke laughed and shook his head. 'OK, so Jess is looking for dog attacks. I'll go grab the books on mythology and demons. Maybe in the demon stuff I'll find something about the Order.'

'I think I'll focus on portals. Those things have to be coming through the one at Mal's place – I mean, the Medway mansion.' That arch looked like it had been there for hundreds of years, way before Mal showed up at school. Malphas. The demon Malphas. Eve didn't like thinking about him as if he were still partly that guy she'd gone so gaga over. She'd even enjoyed just staring at the back of his head when she sat behind him in homeroom. That's how far gone she'd been. Not that she was the only girl in school who'd liked looking at him.

'You OK, Eve?' Jess asked.

'Fine. I was trying to decide if I'd have better luck with the books or searching websites.' She stood up. 'I think I'll start with books. I can go online tonight. I certainly won't be going anywhere, if my mom has anything to say about it.'

She walked over to one of the library terminals.

Hmmm. What subject should she even search for? Hell, she decided. Books that talked about hell might have information about a portal between hell and Earth.

Eve typed in the word, then jotted down a bunch of shelf numbers. By the time she returned to the table, she'd gathered an armload of books. Luke was already back in his seat.

'This library has an amazing amount of material on demons,' he commented.

'Tell me about it,' she agreed as she dumped about a dozen books on the table, then sat down. 'I guess it makes sense with the history of the place.'

'Listen to this,' Luke said. 'It says that hellhounds are lesser demons.'

'Lesser?' Jess repeated. 'They seem pretty evil to me. How many people do they have to kill to get a promotion?'

'Lesser is more about what they feed on.' Luke checked a page of the thick book open in front of him. 'They all get sustenance from the human life force. But higher demons – like Mal – take human souls, while lesser demons go for blood.'

Jess opened a new document and started taking

notes. 'I think it would be good to have everything we find out in one place.'

Luke nodded. 'Go on,' Eve told him. She could tell from the grim look on his face that there was more.

'The hellhounds tear open people's flesh so they can lap up the blood,' he replied. 'That's the part of our life force they live on.'

'I'm glad they didn't get Payne's blood,' Eve said. 'He's been fighting demons all his life. It would be so wrong for them to get life force from him. Not that it isn't horrible that they get it from anyone.'

'Remember to look for anything that sounds like Payne's Order,' Jess commented. 'He recognized the wargs. He knew what they were without having to research. I bet his demon-hunting club could give us a lot of information. And help too.'

'Payne made it sound completely covert, but I'm hoping one of the demonologists who wrote these books will know something about it,' Luke said.

Eve bit her lip. 'Do you think the police will be able to at least find his next of kin to tell them?'

Her friends shrugged, helpless.

'There's a little more on the hellhounds in here.' Luke returned his attention to the book. 'They always hunt in a pack. And they always have one leader – the alpha. Which is the one that can talk.'

'So maybe that's why they all left even though only one of them got hurt,' Eve suggested. 'It must have been the alpha we injured. It was the one that spoke.'

'Makes sense to me,' Luke agreed. 'But you know what I don't get?'

Jess snickered. Eve and Luke looked at her, confused.

'It's just . . . how weird is it that any of us gets any of this?' Jess said.

'True,' Luke said. 'One of the *many* things I don't get is why the wargs just went after Victoria, when we were in the clearing too. It's like they were only hunting her.'

'Maybe that's why the warg was at cheerleading practice. Maybe it was looking for Vic there!' Jess exclaimed.

'Yeah. They only turned on Payne when he attacked them. Same with us.' Eve thought for a moment, trying to recall every detail of the night before. 'They definitely could have come after us.' The idea made her stomach start twisting itself into a pretzel.

Jess continued entering info into her laptop. 'I wonder if that means that the demons picked Ms Taylor and Kyle too. Maybe they can tell whose blood will give them more juice or something.'

'Maybe.' Luke stared up at the ceiling for a moment. 'But why would Kyle, Victoria and Ms Taylor have a stronger life force? Or do you think everyone has the same life force, and the demons were targeting them for a different reason?' A light breeze came through the door, flipping the pages of his book. 'I'm going to shut that.'

He stood up, then sat back down.

'Change your mind?' Jess asked.

'Got an idea.' Luke pulled another bunch of papers out of his backpack. He did a quick glance around the library. Their section was still deserted. 'I brought everything we found in the church that I've been able to translate so far.' He flipped through the papers and set one in the middle of the table.

A wave of dizziness swept through Eve. It was a sketch of the arch, with those markings only she could read. 'You guys still can't . . .' Eve let her words trail off.

'No,' Luke said.

Jess shook her head. 'You're the chosen one, remember?' she said. 'We're your support team. I'm hair, make-up and wardrobe.'

'And I appreciate it,' Eve told her.

'Read what it says on the arch again,' Luke requested.

Eve leaned closer. 'On the hundred-year mark, thy hand or thy blood must the portal open.'

'When I said I was going to shut the door, it started me thinking. On the arch it says the portal must open every hundred years, right?' Luke didn't wait for them to answer. 'And that implies that it's closed the rest of the time.'

'Right,' Eve agreed. 'Because why would you have to open something that was open all the time?'

'Exactly.' Luke slapped the table.

'The portal hasn't been closed though. That's how the hell beasties are coming in,' Jess realized. 'Shouldn't it have been closed after Mal got dusted? He got his chance for this hundred years. He came through. He failed. So why isn't the door closed?'

'OK, it said "thy hand or thy blood". That sounds like only a specific person can open the portal. Probably only the same person can close it,' Luke offered.

'Sometimes I can't believe we talk about all this stuff like it's real,' Eve said.

'It is real,' Luke reminded her.

'I know. But it's also crazy. Isn't it crazy?' she asked.

'Completely crazy,' Jess agreed. 'What does that "thy blood" even mean? Does it take some kind of blood sacrifice to open the thing?'

They all sat in silence, thinking. 'Maybe bloodline?' Eve suggested. 'It's old-fashioned language, like in Shakespeare.' They'd been reading *Julius Caesar* in English. 'Blood can mean family. So the door is opened – and closed – by this specific person or by someone related to him or her.'

'Good call,' Luke said. 'So our portal-closer went to sleep on the job. Maybe they don't know Mal has been dusted. Or maybe something happened to them so they couldn't shut it.'

'So who are we looking for then?' Jess asked. 'Who is the "thy blood"? We have to find whoever it is and get them to slam the portal closed.'

Eve dropped her head into her hands. 'It could be anyone,' she moaned. 'And people are going to keep getting killed until we figure it out.' She raised her head. This wasn't the time to go all dramatic. It was the time to stay calm and think. 'The first owner of the mansion was a Medway,' she said. 'They were a *Mayflower* family. That means they came over from England as pilgrims back in 1620. Maybe a Medway has owned that land for hundreds of years. We know

Deepdene's been a town – or a village at least – for a long time, way before the US was the US. It used to be called Demondene though. Who would move into a place with a name like that?'

'I'm on it.' Jess's fingers flew across her keyboard.

'Just because the arch is on Medway land, doesn't mean a Medway was the original portal-opener,' Luke said.

'I know,' Eve answered. 'But we have to start someplace, and I don't think we have anything else to go on.'

'Gotcha!' Jess exclaimed. She tilted her laptop towards Eve. A scan of a deed filled the screen.

'Wilson Medway bought the land in 1621,' Eve said.

'Problem,' Jess informed them. 'There aren't any Medways in town any more.'

'Someone opened the door, so there has to be a Medway somewhere, even if not right in town,' Luke replied.

'OK. Then we have a plan,' Eve said, feeling a burst of love for her support team. 'Find this Medway descendant before anything else horrible happens in Deepdene.'

Chapter Twelve

Luke rang Eve's doorbell later that night, feeling like a ten-year-old because his dad had driven him. He glanced over his shoulder. His father was still waiting, parked at the curb. He was in hyper-protective mode, making sure that Luke actually made it across the threshold.

What would he do if he knew what was really going on in Deepdene? Luke wondered. *Start carrying me around in a Snugli?* He smiled at the picture.

Eve opened the door. She was wearing a floaty pale blue shirt. It looked so soft he was tempted to run his finger down her sleeve. *Admit it, it's not the shirt you want to touch, it's her*, Luke told himself.

He didn't know exactly when it had happened. Maybe only a few days ago, when Eve wrapped herself around him so tightly after they heard about Ms Taylor's death. Maybe way back on that very first day he ever teased her – about her vanilla-scented lip gloss, he remembered. He was pretty sure that, at least for a moment that day, standing in front of her locker with her, he'd had this crazy urge to kiss her.

No matter when exactly it started, Luke had definitely ended up with some feelings, some more than just friendly feelings, for Eve. He wondered what she'd say if he asked her out.

'Are you coming in? Or are you going to stare some more?' Eve teased him.

Luke shook his head. 'I was just letting my dad see that I'm being allowed in.' He turned and waved, and his dad slowly drove off.

'He's never letting you outside until they catch the animal, right?' Eve asked.

'Yeah. I didn't know he could be more worried than he already was, but he managed it,' Luke said as he stepped into the house.

'Same with my parents,' Eve said. 'Like it's not bad enough that we have demons to deal with, now we have to save the social life of Deepdene too.'

'And convince our parents that this fictional animal is gone,' Luke added.

Eve smiled. 'Jess is already here. We're up in my room. Come on.' She led the way up the stairs.

'Luke! Yay! You're here!' Jess cried when he sat down in the chair in front of Eve's desk. Luke grinned. Sometimes Jess was like a puppy. It had only been about four hours since she saw him last, but she'd given him a first-day-back-at-school greeting.

'I'm here! Hi!' he exclaimed. 'Wassup, girlfriend?'

'Evie has a present for you!' Jess exclaimed.

'Jess . . .' Eve playfully shook her finger at her friend. 'What part of "secret" was confusing to you?'

Luke raised his eyebrows. 'A present?'

Eve pulled a large box out from under her bed and handed it to him. He gave it a shake. No rattle. More of a soft shhhh.

'He's like a little boy at Christmas,' Jess joked.

What could Eve have decided to give him? Only one way to find out. He opened the box. A layer of crisply folded tissue paper blocked his view. He did not even want to think about how much she'd spent. He had to remind himself that money wasn't the same for Eve and Jess and their families as it was for him and his dad.

Luke peeled the tissue away and gave a snort of laughter. A blazer. Eve had gotten him a replacement for the jacket she'd torched.

'It's from 7 for All Mankind. Contemporary fit.

Mid-weight cotton Oxford. Very nice. Very you, I think,' Jess told him. 'And that grey-blue colour – I think Eve made the perfect choice.'

'I hope you like it,' Eve said. 'I convinced my mom that we could squeeze in a ten-minute shopping stop on Main Street on the way home from the library.'

He slipped it on. 'It's great. Might look a little better if it had a scorch mark on the sleeve or something. Can you work on that?' he asked her.

'Just stay close, and I'm sure it'll happen,' she answered.

'I have a present for you too. Kind of.' Luke opened his backpack and pulled out a big stack of large envelopes stuffed with papers. 'These are records from the church, which, as one of the first buildings in Deepdene, has been around for hundreds of years. There's tons of stuff about births, deaths and marriages.' He passed out the envelopes. 'The good news is, the info that we need to find Medway's descendant is probably somewhere in here. The bad news is, it's not organized very well at all.'

'It's better than nothing,' Eve said, opening one of her envelopes.

Luke opened the top one in his pile. The smell of old paper rose out of it. He gently removed what turned out to be a stack of birth certificates. 'If you find anything, shout,' he said. 'We can piece together a Medway family tree.'

They began to work in silence. 'I have a Mattie Dee Medway marrying Bertram DeGroff in 1782,' Eve volunteered.

'Mattie Dee and Bertram. Love those names,' Jess commented.

Luke jotted down a note for the tree. 'OK, so there could be a DeGroff somewhere who is a descendant of our Mr Medway.'

'*Lord* Medway,' Eve corrected him. 'That's what it said on the deed for the land.'

'There are no DeGroffs in town that I can think of,' Jess said. 'We can check the phone book.'

'I can get it online. OK if I use your computer?' Luke asked Eve.

'Sure,' she said.

'Just don't read Evie's email while you're on there,' Jess teased. 'It's full of love notes.'

Eve threw a pillow at Jess, and they both laughed. Luke didn't answer. Was Jess serious? Eve *was* really popular, and Luke had noticed the way guys vied for her attention. How many of them were trying to go out with her?

You know what? Luke told himself. *Think about that once you've found the person who can close the portal.* He turned to Eve's computer and quickly checked for DeGroffs in Deepdene. 'No DeGroffs,' he announced.

'We don't know for sure that the person we're looking for actually lives in Deepdene. I keep forgetting that,' Eve said. 'There are a ton of other towns nearby.'

'All the attacks have been in Deepdene,' Jess said. 'And the portal is here. And Mal went to Deepdene High. It seems like there's serious demon loyalty to this village.'

'It was named Demondene back in the day for a reason. I guess demons like to vacation in the Hamptons too,' Luke said. 'Let's keep working on the assumption that we're looking for someone in Deepdene for now. We can go wider if we have to, but we know for sure somebody was in town last month to open the portal.' They all returned to sorting through the papers.

'There are Coles on our tree, right?' Jess asked a couple of hours later.

Luke consulted the rough family tree – one with lots of missing branches – he'd pulled together. 'Yeah. One of Lord Medway's granddaughters, Ruth Alice

Medway, married a guy called Fred Cole,' he answered. 'You got something?'

'I have a Lisa Cole who married Alex Groshart in 1962,' Jess said.

'Groshart?' Eve exclaimed. 'There are definitely Grosharts here!'

'I know!' Jess waved the marriage certificate in her hand. 'Helena Groshart.'

'And Helena's mom's name was Lisa. I remember from her obituary,' Eve said.

'Yay us! All right!' Jess cheered.

'Whoop!' Eve added, flopping back onto her bed, where she and Jess had been sitting while they worked.

Jess flopped back too. 'We found the descendant. Poor girl. I completely understand how Helena forgot to close the portal. Her mom died a few weeks ago, and then look what happened to Kyle . . .'

Eve wiggled one finger at Luke without sitting up. 'Get over here! We all deserve a rest.'

Luke got up, moved some papers and found a spot to lie down on the bed. 'So we have to talk to Helena.' It was a little difficult to keep his mind on the demon situation. He was on Eve's bed, breathing in the spicy, flowery scent of the perfume she always wore. He couldn't help imagining her in the bed, with all her amazing curls tousled by sleep. She probably . . . He got his brain back under his control. 'Should we call her now?'

'No. This is definitely a face-to-face kind of conversation,' Eve said. She looked at the clock. 'It's almost nine. Let's wait until tomorrow. My mom will have too many questions if I ask her to drive me over there now. And there's no way she'll let me walk, even if all three of us were going together.'

'We've done enough for today,' Jess proclaimed. 'I declare it chill time. Let's order some pizza, watch some movies, eat some Cherry Garcia ice cream. You have Cherry Garcia, right?'

'Of course,' Eve answered. 'You should sleep over.'

'Slumber party!' Jess gave a fist pump. 'I'm so there!' Sometimes it was very easy to remember that Jess was a cheerleader. Luke liked that about her.

Eve sat up and looked over at him. 'You too, Luke. We can set up sleeping bags in the living room.'

Heat washed through Luke's body. This was . . . something. Eve wouldn't invite him to stay over unless she kind of liked him, would she? Well, obviously she liked him. She'd gone out and gotten him a present.

The demon fighting had brought the three of them really close really fast. But this was different. This wasn't demon-related. It was social. Eve wanted to hang with him. So maybe if he asked her out, she'd say yes.

'Do you really want me here, at a girly slumber party?' he joked.

'Of course we want you,' Eve replied, and Luke got that heat rush again. 'You're an honorary girl.'

An honorary girl? The heat drained from his body. *Face reality*, he told himself. *I might want to be more than friends with Eve, but she doesn't think of me as anything more than a pal. Practically a gal pal, for godssake.*

He shoved himself up from the bed. 'No, thanks. I've got nothing to say about nail polish or shoes. I wouldn't be any fun.'

He saw a flash of hurt cross Eve's face. He *had* been a little harsh. But so what? He took his cell out. 'I'll call my dad to pick me up.'

Eve stuck her iPhone in her pocket as she and Jess started down the steps of her front porch late the next morning. Their parents had agreed the two of them could walk over to Helena's as long as they stayed together and got themselves home well before dark. All the attacks had been at night, so most people were willing to ease up on the rules ever so slightly during the day.

'What did Luke say? Is he going to meet up with us so we can all talk to Helena together?' Jess asked.

'No.' Eve shoved her hair behind her ears.

'Why not?' Jess asked.

'Why not?' Eve repeated. 'Because he has something more important to do. He has a date with Briony.'

'He said that was more important?' Jess exclaimed.

'He didn't have to say it. He made his choice,' Eve said testily. She'd thought something was starting up with Luke. Wrong. The holding hands, the hugging – that had only happened because they had been in some extreme situations together. It had been about support and comfort, not anything more.

Just as well, she thought. *Luke's a player. That's not going to change. Even if he was interested in me, it would only have been for a week or two.*

She let out a sigh. 'So how do we do this?' she asked as they walked. 'We can't just say, "Hi, Helena, we've noticed there are some demons around. Did you maybe forget to close the portal?" '

'I guess not,' Jess agreed. 'She might have no idea

about the portal. There might be another descendant who opened it.'

'I hate that we have to talk to her about it at all,' Eve admitted. 'She's gone through so much, losing her mom and Kyle less than a month apart.'

'It's strange to see Helena so quiet and sombre,' Jess said. 'She was the captain of the cheerleading squad for a reason. She was just up, up, up all the time, with all this pep and energy.'

'I can't believe the school didn't give her a break and at least let her stay on the squad,' Eve commented.

'The policy is, you have a D in a class, you're off. And Helena's algebra grade . . .' Jess shook her head. 'But she was scraping by with a C before her mom died. I think the principal, and Ms Taylor, and our coach should have worked out some kind of exception. At least given her a little time to pull the grade up before they kicked her off the team.'

'Lame. So many bad things have happened to her, and they went ahead and took away something that made her happy,' Eve said.

'So happy,' Jess agreed. 'When the coach announced that she'd chosen Helena as head cheerleader, it was like Helena was half-firefly. She glowed. Really. Happiness was shining out of her.'

She stopped walking, and Eve realized they'd already reached Helena's house. This was one of those times she wished Deepdene was a little bigger. She could have used more time to figure out the best way to approach this talk.

'Ready?' Jess asked.

'I guess.' Eve and Jess followed the path that ran through the garden to the front door. Eve hesitated a second, then knocked. No turning back now.

Helena opened the door almost immediately. 'I'm so glad you two called and said you wanted to come by.'

She looked much better than she had the last time Eve had seen her. Of course, that had been at Kyle's funeral. Helena hadn't been to school since, and there were still rumours about her being suicidal. But Helena's cheeks were pink, her hair was shiny and she had a smile on her face – a real smile, not a duty smile. 'Come on in,' she urged.

'How're you doing?' Jess asked. 'You seem a little better.'

'I am,' Helena agreed. 'I'm going back to school tomorrow. I'm ready. I miss people! That's why I'm so glad you girlies came to visit.' Helena sounded a lot like her old cheerleader self, even if she wasn't a cheerleader any more.

'Come on in. I went overboard on the snacks. We can feast.' Helena ushered Eve and Jess into the living room.

'You weren't kidding,' Jess said, taking in the bowls of popcorn, M&Ms, pistachios, veggies and dip.

'Where's your dad?' Eve asked.

'Oh, he's out of town,' Helena said cheerfully. 'He travels for work a lot.'

Eve took a seat on the couch and nibbled on a stick of celery. *I've got to do it*, Eve thought. *I've got to ask her about the portal. But how – really, how – do I start a conversation like that?*

'Helena, would you think I was crazy if . . .' Eve paused, then rushed on. 'Would you think I was crazy if I wanted to talk to you about Lord Medway, and demons and . . . and portals to hell?' Jess choked on an M&M, and Eve shot her an apologetic look. It definitely hadn't been an elegant approach, but at least it was out there.

Eve braced herself, ready for Helena to laugh or to say that yes, she would definitely think Eve was crazy.

Helena's green eyes widened. 'You know about that too?' she exclaimed. 'My mom told me it was a secret. But if you know about it, then it obviously isn't.'

Hmm. I guess honesty is always the best way to go,

Eve thought. She hadn't expected Helena to be quite so quick to talk about this.

'We do know,' Jess said. 'But we don't know a lot.'

'We know that there's this portal that has to be opened every hundred years by a descendant of Lord Medway,' Eve began.

'Uh-huh. I guess it's OK for me to talk about it, if it isn't a secret after all. When my mom first told me our family had this sacred duty to allow demons through the portal, I was all – "not me",' Helena said, grabbing a handful of chips. 'But it turned out to be no big deal. I shut the portal because I knew my mom would want me to. We had this whole talk about it a couple of years ago. She wanted me to know what to do with the portal, if she couldn't.'

She let out a quavery sigh. 'Neither of us thought I'd really need to do anything. My mom was only thirty-seven. Who thought she'd have a heart attack? She opened it before she died though, so I only had to close it.'

Now Eve felt awkward. She definitely couldn't be all, *So, Helena, was your dead mother an evil sociopath? Cos I'm having trouble coming up with another reason why she'd open a portal to hell.*

'Why did she do it?' She asked. 'The portal's a doorway to hell.'

Helena nodded several times. 'I know. My mom hated opening it. She couldn't sleep for weeks before she was supposed to do it. But there's this pact Lord Medway made with a demon. If my mother broke it by not opening the portal, Deepdene would pretty much have had every natural disaster there is coming down on it.'

Helena busied herself piling the chips on a napkin, a lot of the animation draining out of her. 'We talked about it, and my mom thought letting the demons in for a little while was better. She really hated it though.' Helena blinked away tears. 'I wish she'd been happier right before she died.'

Eve blinked. All this information had come spilling out, and Helena hadn't even bothered asking how Eve and Jess knew about the Medways and the portal to hell.

Jess put her hand over Helena's. 'I'm so sorry about your mother. About Kyle too.' She looked over at Eve, and Eve knew Jess was as confused as she was. How had the hellhounds gotten out? She guessed it was possible that they'd slipped through in the time between Mal – the demon

Malphas – died and when Helena closed the portal.

'Thanks,' Helena said. 'Anyway, I did what she asked. I don't understand it at all. I don't even know if the whole thing is even real. Come on – demons?' She popped a chip in her mouth, the moment of sadness passing.

'But you shut it?' Eve said.

'I guess. I did it exactly the way she told me. Mostly I just had to say this incantation and burn a little of my hair,' Helena answered. 'I figured it was some old superstition that her family had, so I would honour it.'

Eve couldn't believe how casual she was about the whole thing. Maybe because she couldn't accept that demons were real. Eve probably wouldn't have been able to either, if she hadn't gotten her powers, turned multiple demons to smoke and faced off with a talking hellhound.

But Helena needed to know the real deal about demons now, although it would make Kyle's death even more painful once she knew he'd been killed by something that came through that portal. And Helena had started to feel better. Still, Eve wanted Helena to be safe, and since she was directly connected to the portal, she should know the truth.

'Helena, I need to tell you – it looks like something came through the portal before you closed it,' Eve said. 'You're sure you closed it, aren't you?'

'Yeah. I had to cut my palm as part of the weird ceremony. As soon as I finished, the cut closed right up.' She held her right palm out for Eve to see. 'My mom said that's how I'd know everything was OK.' Helena frowned. 'Are you saying some kind of demon thingy came here?'

'Lesser demons,' Jess said quickly. 'They're hell-hounds, basically mutant dogs, big black dogs with demon faces.'

'Wait,' Helena said. 'Vic told me she got attacked by dogs like that, and that you guys saved her. I thought her imagination just got out of control because so many awful things had happened. I figured it was just some regular dogs and that you chased them off for her.'

'It wasn't her imagination. And they definitely weren't regular dogs,' Jess said.

'They're called wargs,' Eve added, 'and they're demons. We think they came through the portal before you closed it.'

Helena pressed her fingers to her lips. 'Are they . . . ? They're what killed Kyle, aren't they? And Ms Taylor and that reporter. They're the wild animals that none of the scientists could identify from the bites and claw marks.'

'Yes,' Eve answered simply. There was nothing she could say to make it less horrific or tragic.

They all sat silently for a long moment. Nobody touched the food.

'Be careful, OK, Helena?' Jess finally said, her eyes solemn. 'It's really important to be careful. And don't mention this to anyone else.'

'The wargs seem to target specific people,' Eve explained. 'We don't know why. But you have a connection to the portal. That means you might be on their radar.'

'I've been careful so far. I definitely don't go near the woods or anywhere after dark. My dad's been having me check in every day until he gets back into town too,' Helena said.

'Good. That's good,' Eve said. She just hoped that it would be enough.

Chapter Thirteen

'It still feels so weird to be in bio and not have Kyle there,' Eve told Jess on Monday at school as they headed to the cafeteria.

'It's two weeks ago today that he died,' Jess said.

'I wish I hadn't been so harsh when I turned him down for coffee that last day I saw him.' Eve nibbled on her bottom lip, tasting the vanilla in her lip gloss.

'You have to stop thinking about that,' Jess scolded. 'First, I know you, and I know that you couldn't possibly have been harsh. Firm, yes. Harsh, no. And second, Kyle shouldn't have been asking you or any other girl out when he was with Helena. It's awful that he's dead, but the rules of dating don't change because of that.'

'Eve! Jess! Here I am.' Eve looked over her shoulder and saw Helena coming down the hall towards them with Katy Emory and Belinda Delaware. 'I told you I'd be back today.'

Eve shot a no-more-Kyle-talk look at Jess, and Jess nodded. 'Hey, Helena. How does it feel – being back?' she asked as they all began walking together.

'Good. Really good,' Helena answered. She threw one arm round Belinda's shoulders, the other over Katy's. 'I needed my girls around me.'

'We're sooo glad you're back,' Katy told her. 'And you look fab!'

'You do,' Eve agreed. She was relieved. She'd thought maybe Helena would spiral down again after learning that it was demons who killed Kyle, demons that were still out there somewhere.

'You should be back in cheerleading too,' Belinda said. 'It's so wrong that you're off the squad. And Vic – at the game against St Anthony's the other week she was so wobbly on two lifts I was embarrassed to go to this school.'

'Belinda!' Jess cried.

'I'm calling it like I see it,' Belinda retorted. '*You* were great, Jess.'

'Jess is always awesome,' Helena put in.

'Bee, Vic's been cheerleading since middle school, same as me and Helena. She's gone to cheer camp three times. She's an amazing cheerleader,' Jess said. 'I get that you don't think she deserves to be captain because Helena was the first pick. But don't take it out on Vic, please.'

'Jess is right.' Katy flicked a couple of the locks on the lockers they passed. 'We're still just mad because it wasn't fair for Helena to get kicked out of cheer-leading, with, you know, all the stuff that's been going on.'

'I suppose,' Belinda said grudgingly. 'Hey, was anyone else a hostage this weekend? My parents wouldn't let me out of their sight. They practically escorted me to the bathroom and waited outside the door.'

'My dad's out of town for a few more days,' Helena replied. 'I think he's more worried about my grades than he is about the fact that there's some wild animal in the woods.' She gave Eve a pointed look as she said the word 'animal'.

'My mother is completely grades obsessed,' Eve commiserated as they took their places in the cafeteria food line. 'It's going to be all-you-have-to-think-about-is-college from now until my applications are in – in three years time.'

'Oooh, the romance continues,' Katy whispered.

She jerked her chin towards a table halfway across the room. 'Supposedly Luke and Briony were all *cosy* yesterday afternoon at Piscatelli's. Shanna was there with her family – her parents make all of them go everywhere together now – and she said Luke was feeding Briony a piece of pizza.'

Jess shot a concerned glance at Eve. Eve gave her a shrug to show it was nothing. She shot a look over at Luke. He was leaning towards Briony, listening to her as if he'd never heard anything as interesting as whatever she was saying. Then they both laughed. Eve felt a little itch in her heart, and promised herself not to look at the two of them again for the rest of lunch.

'I've never had a guy feed me,' Belinda complained. 'It always looks so romantic in movies.'

'I always think it means the guy is a control freak,' Eve said. 'I mean, what if she didn't even want pizza?'

They all stared at her for a minute. Then Belinda laughed. 'You're right. Things always look more exciting in the movies.'

'I don't know. I think it's plenty exciting around here lately,' Katy put in. 'Except it's more like a horror movie.'

Eve paid for her spinach salad and Diet Coke. After Helena paid for her lunch Eve managed to pull her aside for a moment. 'Thanks for not talking about the *thing*. If everybody knew, there'd be mass panic.'

'It's my secret too,' Helena answered. 'I only talked about it with you and Jess because you already knew.' She smiled. 'I'm so glad that I have a couple of people I can talk to about everything. It's all so weird.'

'Way too weird to deal with alone.' Eve squeezed Helena's hand. 'I know it's been really hard for you lately,' she added, 'but things are going to get better.'

'They will,' Helena agreed. 'They already are, at least a little. Partly thanks to you.'

Eve leaned deeper into the overstuffed couch in Jess's living room and stretched her arms above her head. She, Jess and Luke had been meeting up every day after school to research and strategize. It was Wednesday, day three, and they still hadn't come up with much. Luke had actually found a reference to the thirteen swords that could kill demons. They were supposed to have been forged by Lucifer, back when he was still an angel. The article hadn't mentioned where any of the swords might be now though.

He looked up from the map spread across the coffee table. 'I'm having no luck figuring out where the wargs are hiding, since we know they aren't going back and forth through the portal.'

See, it's all fine with him, Eve told herself, as she'd been telling herself every time they were together post-him-going-out-with-Briony. *Me, Jess and Luke working on stopping the badness, same as always. No weirdness between us, because we're just friends.*

'Well, I'm having no luck finding out anything more about Payne's demon-hunting order,' Jess said, without looking up from her laptop. 'Not even a mention.'

'Let's go back to trying to figure out the connection between Victoria, Ms Taylor and Kyle,' Eve suggested. She took a sip of her Jones cherry soda. 'We saw how the hellhounds targeted Vic. They weren't interested in us or Payne at all until we started fighting them. So Ms Taylor and Kyle probably weren't random victims either. Why would the demon dogs choose those three people in particular?'

'The wargs drink blood,' Luke said. 'Maybe we should try to check the medical records of the victims. Maybe they are a rare blood type, or all had an elevated level of some kind of hormone. Dogs could probably smell something like that. They have an awesome sense of smell. The demon dogs probably do too.'

'Look at the brain on Luke,' Jess joked.

'He's a little bit of a star in biology,' Eve told her. Thinking of biology made her think of Kyle. Why couldn't she let go of the guilt? *She* wasn't the one who had been attempting to cheat on Helena. 'Helena!' she exclaimed.

'Helena?' Jess echoed. 'What about her?'

'She was Kyle's girlfriend. And she was in Ms Taylor's class,' Eve started.

Jess jumped in. 'Oh, and she used to be on the cheerleading squad with Vic.

'Kind of a random bunch of connections,' Luke said.

'But they're still connections, which is more than we've come up with so far,' Eve replied.

'I don't get why hellhounds would care about any of that. Why would hellhounds especially want to kill people Helena knows?' Jess asked.

'Because Helena is the person who can open and shut the portal,' Eve guessed. 'That can't be a coincidence.'

'Good point.' Luke began folding up the map. 'We don't know anything about how the Medways first got into the portal business. But we know they have been dealing with demons in some way for hundreds of years.'

'Maybe the wargs are attacking people close to Helena, people she cares about, to force her to do something for them,' Eve suggested, although she couldn't think of what exactly they might want.

'Helena didn't say anything to us about that,' Jess reminded her.

'Yeah, but Helena was weird about the whole portal and demon thing,' Eve said. 'She was really casual about it. It didn't seem like she knew much more than how to shut it. Maybe there are other things a Medway can do that her mom didn't get the chance to tell her about.'

'Maybe they want the portal opened again,' Luke suggested. 'Maybe they want more hellhounds to be able to come through.'

Eve felt as if someone were squeezing her ribcage. 'Or other kinds of demons. Maybe even the higher kinds, the ones who feed on souls, like Mal.'

'We've got to call Helena right away,' Luke said. 'She needs to know that the wargs could be targeting people that mean something to her.'

'And that they might be targeting her too!' Eve reached into her bag and pulled out her iPhone. Before she could open her contacts, the phone began to vibrate in her hand. 'Freaky. It's Helena,' Eve said.

She hit 'answer'. Helena started talking before Eve even had the chance to say hello. 'Eve, those demons, the hellhounds – they're here. They're right outside my house! I don't know what to do. What am I supposed to do?' Her voice rose into a scream.

'I'm coming over. Just stay inside. Go in a room without any windows and don't move.' Eve hung up and leaped to her feet. 'The hellhounds are at Helena's,' she cried.

'Should we call the police?' Jess asked, jumping up.

'They can't kill demons,' Luke said. Then he stopped and grimaced. 'Crap. I don't have the sword. I came straight from school, and I can't wear it there because of gym.'

'It doesn't matter. I can kill demons,' Eve said.

'But you need help. We need the sword,' Luke burst out. 'We have to go get it.'

Eve shook her head. 'I'm going straight to Helena's.'

'Me too,' Jess said. 'Those dogs are at her house!'

'I wish you'd wait,' Luke began, then seemed to realize he wouldn't change their minds. 'I'll be there as fast as I can.'

'Good.' Eve felt a rush of relief at the thought. She

might be the Deepdene Witch, but that didn't mean a guy with a demon-killing sword wouldn't come in handy. Especially if that guy was Luke.

Chapter Fourteen

'Jess, will you please just go back home?' Eve pleaded as they raced towards Helena's.

Jess didn't answer, but she kept running alongside Eve.

'Luke will have the sword,' Eve continued breathlessly. 'I have my witch powers. You won't have anything to protect you.'

Jess didn't answer that one either.

'OK, OK.' There was no way she could force Jess back to her house. It was pretty much impossible to force Jess to do anything. 'But be careful. Please, please be careful.'

They rounded the corner onto Helena's street. Actually it was a private drive. Helena's place was the only house on it, with the woods butting up against one side.

A hideous bellow sounded, turning Eve's blood to

ice-water. *Inspiring terror – check*, Eve thought, remembering what Luke had read to them at the library about the wargs' howls.

She reached out and grabbed Jess's arm. 'We can't just charge up the front walk. We have to figure out where exactly the wargs are.'

Jess nodded. 'Once we do, if there's a way to get to one of the doors, I'll go straight in and find Helena,' she said. 'She has to be scared out of her mind.'

'Perfect.' Jess was right about Helena. And Eve was relieved Jess had a plan that involved getting herself at least partially out of danger.

Slowly Eve and Jess crept down the street. Dusk had slipped into darkness, which would make the black dogs almost impossible to spot. Almost. Eve caught sight of a pair of flame-filled eyes. Then another. And another. Three hellhounds were circling Helena's perfectly manicured front yard. A snake of loathing writhed through Eve as she tracked the glowing orbs, imagining the gruesome demon faces that she couldn't clearly see.

'Maybe the side gate?' Jess suggested.

'Probably as good a way as we're going to find,' Eve agreed. The front gate wasn't an option. A hellhound was positioned in front of it.

'Slow or fast?' Jess asked.

'Let's keep going slow,' Eve answered. 'They probably know we're here. But if we charge the gate they'll absolutely know, and they'll probably get there before we do.'

Head down, crouching low, Eve led the way to the side gate. As she opened it, it gave a metallic screech. *So much for stealth*, Eve thought as all three hellhounds began baying in a soul-searing chorus.

Even worse was the sound of the demons rushing towards her and Jess. Eve pushed Jess towards the porch, then braced her legs apart and thrust her hands out at the first of the hellhounds hurtling towards her.

Her power had completely replenished itself, and it felt eager to spring free. Flame-licked lightning bolts rammed into the chest of the nearest hound. The demon hissed, then shrieked as it turned to smoke that twisted off into the night.

Out of the corner of her eye she saw another hellhound leaping at her from the left. She whirled towards it. She felt the polish on her nails melt as she hurled her power towards the beast. It turned to smoke in mid-air. She caught sight of Helena and Jess on the porch. Helena's mouth was open as she stared in shock. Seeing demons was a lot different to hearing about them.

Eve felt as if her body were made of power. Her bones were lightning bolts. She wouldn't be surprised if her own eyes were glowing. As the third demon flung itself at her, her power shot into it naturally. She was acting on pure instinct, without thought or strain, and it felt awesome.

She checked the yard for more hellhounds, but she had vanquished them all. She pulled in a deep breath, feeling completely, wonderfully, extremely alive. Then she laughed. She could tell Luke that she didn't need him and the sword after all. She had kicked ass.

Eve pulled out her cell and dialled as she started towards Jess and Helena. 'All done,' she announced, giddy with her accomplishment, when Luke picked up. 'There were three of them, and I got them all. Bam, bam, bam! You should have seen me!'

She paused, one foot on the bottom step leading to the porch. 'The Sword of Demon Death isn't needed.' Then she frowned as she felt the ground tremble under her feet. A horrible clicking sound was coming from the direction of the woods.

Eve jerked towards the sound. 'Oh, God, no!' she exclaimed as a pack of wargs exploded from between the thick trees. Their viciously sharp claws sent up sparks as hundreds of the demon dogs raced down the street.

'What? What's happening, Eve?' Luke demanded. The cell slipped from Eve's fingers. They'd gone numb.

'Eve!' Jess was beside her. 'Come on!' She grabbed Eve by the arm and pulled her up the porch stairs to the safety of Helena's house. Helena watched them from the open doorway. When Eve and Jess reached her, she didn't step aside to let them in.

Instead she looked Eve in the eye – and slowly closed the thick oak door right in her face . . . Leaving Eve and Jess exposed as the hundreds of hellhounds approached.

Chapter Fifteen

'Helena!' Jess screeched, pounding on the door with both fists. 'Let us in!'

Eve stared at the closed door, unable to believe what had just happened. A chorus of long bellows jerked her out of her momentary stupor. She spun towards the sound just in time to see the first hellhound in the pack leap over the front fence.

'Helena!' Jess cried again.

'She's not coming,' Eve stated. She positioned her body between Jess and the huge black demon dogs. She could feel her power coiling inside her, ready. But would she have the force to destroy the entire pack? How could she?

A different bellow sounded. Not terror inducing, *hope* inducing. Luke. He let out another war cry as he charged through the side gate, sword drawn and ready. He reached the porch as the first wargs arrived at the centre of the yard.

Eve and Luke exchanged a terrified look. Even together, with the sword and her powers, they were no match for the pack of slavering hellhounds. 'Up!' Luke ordered, sheathing his sword. 'The roof!'

He grabbed Jess and gave her a boost. 'Now you,' he told Eve. He laced his fingers together, and she put her foot in the stirrup he'd formed. As he lifted she threw up both her hands and managed to grab the rain gutter. From somewhere above, Jess took her by the wrists and helped her haul herself the rest of the way onto the roof.

'You may be the Deepdene Witch, but I have the strength and endurance of a cheerleader,' Jess managed to joke.

A few seconds later Luke had joined them. They all stared down at the pack, which had formed a ragged ring around the front of the house. The hundreds of glowing red eyes made Eve feel as if she were looking down into the embers of a bonfire.

'OK, at least now we have time to make a plan,' Luke said. 'Where's Helena? Is she all right?'

'She's fine.' Disgust edged Jess's voice. 'When the hellhounds appeared in the street, she closed the door in our faces. I couldn't believe it!'

Luke frowned. 'Did she know you were out here?'

'Yes! We were about two inches away from her! Maybe she freaked,' Jess cried. 'Maybe she completely freaked and panicked and lost control of herself,' she added, softening.

'She saw you deal with the first wargs, right?' Luke asked Eve. She nodded. 'Maybe she figured that you could handle the pack on your own.'

'No. The way she looked at me . . .' Eve shuddered, remembering the cold fury of Helena's eyes. 'It was like she hated me, like she wanted me to get killed.'

'Why would she hate you?' Jess protested. 'You never did anything to her.'

'I don't know.' Suddenly Eve felt as if someone with an iron fist had punched her in the gut. 'But I know why she would hate Kyle – and Vic!'

'Oh my God, yeah!' Jess exclaimed. 'Vic took her spot as head cheerleader. Getting that spot meant so much to Helena.'

'And Kyle asked me out right before he died. He was always flirting with other girls even though he and Helena were together,' Eve added. 'Maybe that's why she hates me.'

'Kyle asked you out?' Luke said sharply, then he shook his head. 'Never mind. What about Ms Taylor though? How does her death fit?' Eve concentrated on his eyes, looking only at them. Looking down, into the hideous faces of the demons with their maws gaping, made her feel as if the roof were pitching and rolling under her feet.

'You know, Ms Taylor's kind of the one who got Helena kicked off the squad in the first place,' Jess said slowly. 'She refused to pass Helena in algebra. If Helena hadn't been getting a D in Ms Taylor's class, she'd still be head cheerleader.'

'That's not exactly Ms Taylor's fault,' Luke said.

'Helena could feel like it was though,' Jess answered.

Eve's brain kept trying to reject the conclusion she was coming to. It was too evil. But it also made a horrible kind of sense. 'Could Helena be controlling them somehow?' she asked, flicking her eyes towards the hellhounds. 'Could she have *used* them to kill Kyle and the others?'

'On purpose?' Jess cried. 'But . . . but it's Helena.'

'The Medways have this long history with demons,' Luke said. 'We don't know most of it. Like why did Lord Medway ever agree to open the portal and let demons in? Maybe they—'

'Listen,' Jess whispered.

For a moment Eve didn't know what she was supposed to be listening to. Then she realized the hellhounds had fallen completely silent. Her ears still ringing from the bellowing, Eve took another look down at the demon dogs.

Her heart skittered. Helena had joined them out on the front lawn. Every demon's eyes were turned towards her, the red-orange fires burning bright as they focused on the slim pretty girl who wasn't much taller than they were.

Helena gave Luke, Jess and Eve a friendly wave. 'You'll have to come down sometime,' she said in a singsong. Then her eyes narrowed on Eve. 'Is there something you want to tell me, Eve Evergold?' Her voice had lost all its playfulness. Now it was coated with malice and cold anger.

'*I've* got something to tell you,' Jess shouted. 'You're a complete psycho! I mean, look at your little pets. Look at them! They're monsters.'

'They're wonderful. So loyal.' Helena stroked the black cheek of the warg that sat closest to her. It grinned up at her. The sight started acid churning in Eve's stomach.

'I was expecting Malphas at the portal on All Hallow's Eve,' Helena continued. 'That's when he had to go back, and I was supposed to shut the portal behind him.'

She played us perfectly that day we came to visit her, acting like she hardly knew anything about demons, Eve thought.

'I was planning to renegotiate the pact,' Helena said. 'Maybe let Malphas stay a little longer if he agreed to do me a few favours. He didn't show.' Helena raised one eyebrow. 'I suspect the reason has something to do with Miss Zappy Fingers up there.'

'Oh my God, you lied to us!' Jess exclaimed. 'You never shut the portal, did you? You let those things out on purpose! They've been going back and forth whenever they want. That's why the police and all those animal people never found them.'

'Good to see you've caught up,' Helena answered. 'Why would I close it? I wouldn't have my beauties if I did.' She smiled at the hellhounds.

'Malphas is a demon. And so are those fiends you like so much,' Luke shouted down. 'Don't you have any concept of what that means?'

Helena laughed. 'Typical minister's son,' she scoffed. 'So worried about right and wrong. But you also have to know the power demons possess. And I can have that power, because I control the portal. The demons need me.'

One of the hellhounds gave a sharp bark as if it

agreed. 'As it turns out, it didn't really matter that I couldn't make a new arrangement with Malphas,' Helena continued. 'These lovelies were on the other side of the portal – they're guardians between the worlds, you know – and we made a deal of our own. I agreed to leave it open so they could come in and feed. And in return they agreed to let me choose who they fed on.'

'That's disgusting!' Jess exclaimed.

'Only because you care about being a good girl.' Helena smiled. 'You should try being a bad one. It's a lot more fun.'

'What you're doing isn't bad. It's evil,' Luke told her.

'I'm bored,' Helena said, 'and the wind is messing up my hair. I'm going inside.'

A few of the wargs whined. 'They're hungry,' Helena said. She locked eyes with Eve. 'And you're dinner.'

'No!' Jess cried.

'She deserves it,' Helena said. 'Just like the others. She was trying to steal Kyle away from me.'

Before Eve could protest, Helena turned her attention to the demon dogs. 'OK, babies, time to eat,' she crooned. She pointed up at Eve. 'Kill her!'

Chapter Sixteen

'Helena was right about one thing,' Luke said. 'We can't stay up here for ever.'

One of the hellhounds gave an experimental swipe at the side of the house. Its claws grabbed hold briefly, sending out a spray of sparks. 'Even if we could, it looks like *they* might not stay down *there*,' Jess replied. 'They're already trying to figure out how to come and get us.'

'I'm still pretty juiced up,' Eve told them. 'But there are at least a hundred demons down there. I don't think I'll be able to kill them all.' She turned to Luke. 'Even with you backing me up with the sword.' Panic rose inside her, and she struggled to keep it in check. There had to be a way out of this. She just needed to stay calm and think.

She forced herself to look down at the wargs, even though the sight of them repulsed her. They stared back at her avidly, drool dripping down their chins. 'They must have a weakness we can use,' she murmured. She concentrated on remembering every detail of the night in the clearing. There had to be something . . .

'Alpha dog!' she exclaimed.

Luke's eyes brightened. He immediately grasped what she meant. 'Yes!' he exclaimed. 'When the alpha was injured and left the clearing, the other wargs went with it. So we really don't have to fight all of them' – he swept his arm at the waiting hellhounds – 'only the alpha.'

'But how can we tell which one that is? They all look alike.' Jess swallowed hard enough for Eve to hear it. 'And there are so, so many of them.'

'They don't *act* alike. The alpha will be the one that leads the attack. We can use that,' Luke said.

'Um, problem,' Jess said. 'Is it really going to help us to ID the alpha when it's *leading an attack*? Seems a little late to me.'

'The attack won't be on all of us. It will be on me,' Luke said. 'I'll go down there as bait.'

'No!' Eve yelped, her imagination supplying a picture of Luke lying on the ground, his body mauled, the hellhounds lapping up his blood, his life force.

'What else is there to do?' Luke asked. 'Look at all of them. The only way we're going to have a shot is to target the alpha.' He rushed on before Eve could protest. 'I'll go down there. The alpha will lead the attack on me. As soon as it's clear which one it is, you blast it.'

'And afterwards I'll take you home and put a mango-butter hair masque on you. You're getting a little frizz, the way you do when you zap,' Jess offered. Her voice quivered a little, but she managed to smile at Eve.

Eve's heart constricted. Jess was the best best friend imaginable. Eve had to fight demons? Jess was there. Even with no powers of her own to protect her. 'I love you,' she told her friend. 'You too, Luke.'

It was true. Yeah, he was a player. Yeah, he wasn't interested in her like that. But that didn't have anything to do with the kind of love for him that was flooding through her.

'Me too. Both of you,' Luke answered. 'OK, I'm going down there. You ready?' he asked Eve.

'What should I do?' Jess asked. 'Besides the masque when we're done, obviously.'

'*Please* just stay up here, Jess,' Eve pleaded. 'I have to concentrate on bringing down the alpha. I don't want to worry about what's happening to you. And you know I would.'

Jess nodded. 'OK. You've convinced me. I didn't really want to go down there anyway, but I would have if you needed me to. Luke, you have the sword, so it'll be good.'

'Wait!' Eve burst out. 'You can't use the sword – not until we figure out which one is the alpha. If you start off by attacking, all the wargs will attack – just in self-defence. Like they did with Payne. It won't tell us anything.' Thank God she'd realized in time. If Luke was going to put himself in horrible danger, it had to at least be for a good reason.

'I'll wait until the alpha shows itself,' Luke promised. He walked to the far end of the roof, as far as he could get from the pack of hellhounds. None of the demon dogs tracked him. They stood where they were, intently focused on Eve. She crouched down, ready to blast her power as soon as she spotted the alpha. She wasn't sure exactly what the range of the lightning bolts was. Could she even hit the alpha from the roof? She'd just have to hurl the power out with everything she had – and hope.

'Hey, mutts! The dog catcher's here!' Luke yelled, then leaped.

Eve's eyes jerked over the pack. A couple of the wargs turned their heads towards Luke, but none of them made a move. Luke put one hand on the hilt of the sword, but made no move to pull it free. He simply looked at the wargs, waiting.

The demon dogs continued to hold their focus on Eve, their muscles tense with anticipation.

'Uh, hello? Right here!' Luke shouted. 'Come and get me.'

The ear of one warg twitched. That was the only response Eve could see. It was like on Friday night. 'It's like in the clearing. They only cared about Vic, unless someone else was attacking them,' she said.

'Now they only care about you, Eve,' Jess said softly. 'Look at them. They're all staring at you, right at you.'

'Helena tells them who to feed on,' Eve answered. 'She admitted it. That was her deal with the wargs.' Her mouth and throat started to go dry as she spoke the words.

'And Helena ordered to them to ki— to get you. Not Luke,' Jess said. 'That's why they don't care about him.'

'This plan won't work then,' Eve said desperately. 'Maybe I should jump down there. I can try to kill the alpha before it gets to me.'

'It won't work. They're watching the tiniest move you make,' Jess told her. 'The second you even start to jump, they'll pounce. By the time you land, the alpha will be on you already. You won't have time to get your power going.'

'I've got to do *something*,' Eve said.

'Come here.' Jess grabbed Eve's arm and pulled her back, away from the edge of the roof and over to the chimney that rose up from the centre of the house. They couldn't see the hellhounds from here, and judging by the sudden bellowing and barking the hellhounds couldn't see them either. 'I might have an idea,' Jess said. 'Trade coats with me.'

Eve didn't like where it seemed this plan of Jess's was going. 'Jess . . .'

'I can be the bait instead of Luke,' Jess told her. 'In your coat, I'll smell like you.'

'Jess . . .' Eve began again, but Jess wouldn't let her interrupt.

'I know, I know. Those are demons we're dealing with. But they are a lot like dogs, huge scary dogs with huge scary teeth and claws,' Jess continued. 'They aren't that smart. The alpha's a little smarter, but it's taking commands from Helena. How smart can it be?'

Eve gave a snort of laughter – almost hysterical

laughter, but still laughter. It dried up when Jess reached for the zipper on Eve's pink jacket. 'Jess, no—'

'Come on. I promise not to get it dirty,' Jess said. 'Unlike the Zac Posen blouse with the organza collar that you borrowed and spilled salad dressing on.' She put her hands on Eve's shoulders. 'Luke's down there with the sword. You'll be right behind me with your fingers. This is a good idea. It's more than a good idea. It's our best chance.'

Eve tried to think of an alternative plan, but nothing came to her. She slowly unzipped her jacket and traded it for Jess's black sateen one. They turned round and went back to the edge, hand in hand.

'Luke!' Eve called. When he looked up, she pointed to her jacket and then Jess's, hoping he'd understand the new plan.

'I'm coming down,' Jess added. She turned to Eve. 'Don't worry. I'm a cheerleader – strong, flexible and able to scream really loudly.' She illustrated by screaming really loudly as she jumped off the roof.

Eve's heart gave a desperate thump as she watched her best friend fall. She tried to look at all the demon dogs at once, feeling her power pulse inside her, hot and ready. She couldn't think about Jess. She had to find the alpha.

One warg tilted back its head and sniffed the air. Was that it? Was that the alpha?

Her question was answered when the hellhound gave a bellow and ran at Jess. Eve aimed her hands at it. When the lightning bolts burst from her fingers, they were edged with pure blue flames. *This is going to work!* Eve thought.

But before the bolts drove into the alpha, the hellhound leaped into the air, going for Jess's throat. Eve jerked her hands, trying to follow the warg's trajectory. She winced as the bolts hit one of the columns on the porch, but she managed to redirect them in time to strike the alpha on the flank. Eve hadn't killed it, but she'd knocked it off course, throwing it to the ground before it could touch Jess.

Her power churned inside her, molten now. She felt the burn of it, but it didn't bring any pain. Instead it brought strength and energy. Eve aimed her hands at the alpha as it struggled to its feet. 'This time you die,' she muttered.

But just as she threw out her hands she heard a horrible cracking sound. The column she'd hit with her power had snapped in half, and the section of roof under her feet was giving way. Eve was thrown off balance, her power shooting out harmlessly into the air.

She started to slide. She'd landed on her back and was moving fast. In a few seconds she'd reach the edge and plummet to the ground. Eve flipped onto her stomach, then struggled to shove herself to her knees. But before she could, her feet slid all the way off the roof.

Eve tried to dig her fingernails into the shingles, but she couldn't get a grip. Her knees were off the roof now, her thighs, her belly. If she hit the ground, the plan would be ruined. The wargs would get her scent, and it would be so much stronger than the scent coming from the coat Jess was wearing.

Her chest was off now. Her shoulders. But before she dropped to the ground she was able to grab the rain gutter with one hand. She had to get back up on the roof. What was happening with Jess and Luke? Her back was to the yard and she couldn't see them or the wargs.

Eve managed to get her other hand on the rain gutter. She struggled to pull herself up. Why, oh why, hadn't she done more pull-ups in her life?

The gutter buckled, then cracked, and Eve was falling again. She gasped as she hit the ground. Pain raced up one leg, but she ignored it and jumped to her feet. She expected the alpha to come rushing at her, but the whole pack was on the move, galloping across the yard.

Galloping after Jess.

Jess sprinted through the front gate. Luke was right behind her. And the entire pack of hellhounds was right behind them both.

Chapter Seventeen

Eve took off after Luke and Jess. Maybe she could run fast enough to circle around the pack and zap the alpha. She quickly realized that would be impossible. The pack was halfway down the block. Eve's lungs and legs were straining and she was only moving fast enough to keep them in sight.

She couldn't see her friends. There were a hundred hellhounds between her and Luke and Jess. Not knowing what was happening to them made Eve feel crazy with fear. At least Luke had the sword. Eve had sent her best friend into a pack of demons with no protection. What had she been thinking?

And what had Helena been thinking, to let the wargs into their world? How could anyone be so selfish? She'd put the whole town in danger just so she could do things like punish an unfaithful boyfriend. That was more than selfish. Luke was right. It was evil. Helena was as evil as the demons themselves.

Sparks crackled from Eve's fingers as she thought about Helena. She forced her power down. She couldn't waste even a little of it venting her anger at Helena, or at herself for putting Jess's life on the line.

Eve was gaining on the hellhounds now. It took her a few moments to realize that the reason she was closing in on them was because they had stopped. She moved around the side of the pack, straining to see.

'Not good,' she breathed when she spotted Luke with his back pressed against a tree at the edge of the woods. He was whipping the sword from side to side, barely managing to keep the demons a few feet back. Jess was perched in the branches above him. The hellhounds had them cornered, their baying rising to an unholy pitch.

Thank God Luke has the sword, Eve thought. But her mind provided a picture of Payne fighting with that same sword. He was an experienced demon fighter, and a hellhound had killed him. What chance did Luke have?

He has me, Eve reminded herself. *The Deepdene Witch.* And unlike on the night in the clearing, she still had power. She wouldn't let anything happen to Luke and Jess. She would *not.*

She'd reached the front of the pack. They hadn't noticed her. The wind had picked up. Maybe that was keeping her scent from them. Eve could see the alpha. Her lightning bolt had singed the hair off part of its flank. The bare skin, red and sore-looking, was easy to spot against the demon dog's black coat. The creature was positioned right in front of Luke, inches away from the reach of the sword.

Eve raised her hands, flexing them to stop them trembling. She would only have one shot at this. If she missed, the alpha would have the whole pack on her. She took aim.

'Boo!'

Eve dropped her hands and whipped her head towards the sound. Helena had appeared beside her, riding on the back of one of the largest hellhounds. 'This is going to be even more delicious than I thought,' Helena told Eve. 'I get to watch you watch your friends die. And then I get to watch you die yourself. Fun!'

Don't listen to her, Eve told herself. She turned back to the pack. It took her a second to spot the alpha again. When she found it, its head was raised and it was sniffing. Its tongue slipped out and flicked back and forth as though the demon were tasting the air.

Eve's heart gave a painful double thump, then began beating twice as fast as before. She slowly raised her arms, not wanting to draw attention to herself with a sudden motion. As she took aim on the alpha, it turned its head towards her – along with every other hellhound.

They've spotted me, she realized. *They know I'm the one they really want.*

The alpha took a few steps towards Eve, and the entire pack swung round to follow it. Eve's hands were shaking so hard that her aim was jumping from demon to demon. She *had* to hit the alpha.

The alpha's muscles bunched as it broke into a run, kicking up the fallen leaves as it moved faster than it should have been able to, even with its long, powerful legs. Jess gave a shriek of terror. If the alpha killed Eve, it would mean death for Luke and Jess too. Helena wanted them all dead. She'd turn the wargs on them as soon as Eve was taken care of.

Eve narrowed her focus to the two gleaming red orbs that were the alpha's eyes. The beast was so close she could smell its rancid breath. She thrust out her hands, putting every molecule of her body behind the power as she let it fly. The lightning bolts lit up the night. The burst was so strong that the recoil knocked her to the ground.

She scrambled up, searching for the alpha. It lay at her feet, a raw red hole between its eyes. Eve noticed that the fire had gone out of them. They were empty and black now.

'Poor boo-boo.' Helena climbed off her mount and knelt beside the alpha. She stroked its coarse black hair, then looked up at Eve. 'But it doesn't matter. I have lots more.' She rose to her feet and smiled. 'Kill her!' she ordered the pack, pointing at Eve.

Luke reached Eve's side seconds after Helena issued the command. He had his sword at the ready, but the hellhounds didn't move towards Eve. A few sniffed at the fallen alpha. The others wandered aimlessly, moaning and howling.

'Kill her!' Helena shrieked. 'Now!'

The demon dogs turned, but not towards Eve, towards Helena. Many of them were salivating. *They're hungry*, Eve realized with horror.

Helena advanced on the pack, her body tense with anger. 'You heard me. Kill her. Now!'

The wargs began to get twitchy, as if they were agitated by her shrill voice. 'Helena, don't. You're upsetting them,' Eve warned. She kept her own voice calm, although adrenalin was pumping through her.

'Her. Kill *her*. Now, now, now!' With each 'now' Helena jabbed her finger in Eve's direction. 'Now!' she cried again. When she started to make another jab, one of the demons leaped up and caught her arm in its jaws.

That was all it took, one warg moving.

Instantly a feeding frenzy started, with hellhounds biting and clawing at any part of Helena's body they could reach. 'Stop! I'm your master!' Helena wailed.

Chapter Eighteen

Helena screamed again. The sound turned Eve's whole body to gooseflesh. She threw out her hands, aiming at the closest hellhound. She wasn't surprised when only a pale fizzing flicker of lightning left her fingers. That last blast had taken everything out of her.

Jess tugged at Eve's sleeve. 'There's nothing you can do, Evie. We have to go.'

Eve hadn't realized Jess had come down from the tree. Her attention had been riveted by the pack. It was like looking into a pot of boiling black water. The demons were climbing over each other in their fever to get to Helena.

'We can't leave her to be ripped apart by wargs,' Eve protested. 'No matter how evil she is.'

'Jess is right,' Luke said. 'We can't save her. There are too many of them.' He began to back slowly away from the demon dogs, gesturing Eve and Jess to come with him. 'They aren't going to be satisfied with Helena. When they're done, they might turn on us if we're still here. Without their alpha, the pack is unpredictable.'

Eve knew he was right, and she began backing away too, although leaving Helena there felt so wrong. When they were a few paces away from the hell-hounds Luke said, 'I think we're good to run. They aren't going to notice anything until all her blood is gone.'

'Yeah, let's go.' Eve took one last look at the dogs. She couldn't see Helena. The pack was crowded too tightly around her.

Eve turned and ran, Luke and Jess beside her.

Luke kept glancing from Eve to Jess as they ran. He couldn't quite believe they'd all actually escaped from the pack alive. Wild exhilaration filled him, but underneath it he felt a grim, cold sense of doom. When they started to pass Helena's house, he stopped.

'Out of breath already?' Jess teased, panting.

'We have to figure out how to close the portal. And the best chance we have is to search in there.' He jerked his chin at the house.

'You're right. Something new could be coming through right now,' Eve said. 'We need to find out what we can.' Luke had thought she might be freaked out after what they'd just gone through, but she was rock strong. So was Jess.

'Let's do this,' Jess said. 'Then the hair masque. I'll give you one too,' she told Luke. 'Although your hair is already so pretty.' She ruffled his long bangs, and Luke grinned.

'I'd think I'd rather face another demon than whatever a hair masque is,' he told her as he led the way to the house. The collapsed section of roof blocked part of the front door, but it still opened and they managed to squeeze inside.

'Helena's bedroom's down the hall to the left,' Jess announced. 'She had everybody in the squad over for lunch when she made head cheerleader.'

Luke snorted. 'Head cheerleader! People died over who got to be head cheerleader.'

'Head cheerleader is a position of honour, leadership and responsibility,' Jess said. It sounded as if she were quoting something. 'A real head cheerleader would never make a deal with a bunch of disgusting demons.'

'I'm thinking she must have made the deal with the

alpha warg only,' Luke answered. 'The others can't speak, and they aren't as intelligent.'

'That's why it didn't work when she ordered the rest of the hellhounds to kill me,' Eve said. 'They didn't have a bargain with her.'

'Maybe they didn't even understand what she said.' Jess led the way into Helena's room.

'Not what I was expecting,' Eve said. 'It's so . . . normal. I was expecting the Lair of the Warg Queen.'

'That would be in here,' Jess said. She had opened the door of the walk-in closet.

Luke moved closer to look inside. He immediately saw what Jess meant. The free walls and even part of the ceiling were covered with pictures of demons. Fluorescent Post-it notes dotted the images. He stepped into the closet, flicked on the light and read one aloud: '"Lix Tetrax. Controls the four winds! Cool!"' The exclamation points were big and puffy – so girly. 'How could a normal girl do something like what she did?'

Luke pulled the Lix Tetrax picture off the wall. 'I'm taking these. I'm going to start a database with everything we find out about demons. Just in case.'

Eve leaned into the closet. 'I wonder if one of these is what Mal really looked like.'

'Don't think about it. Help me search the room while Luke handles the closet,' Jess said 'I want to find out how to close the portal and get out of here.'

'I'll look on the computer,' Eve answered.

Luke began reading the other Post-its and looking at the pictures to see if one showed something like the arch, taking down the pictures as he went. He needed a chair to get the stuff on the ceiling. 'Any luck?' he asked Eve as he walked out of the closet to fetch one.

She shook her head. She looked exhausted, with dark smudges under her eyes, her shoulders drooping as she sat in front of the computer. Luke moved up behind her and began to massage them. Probably not a good idea. He'd promised himself to stop thinking about Eve *that way*. There was no point, since she only thought of him as a gal pal.

That's why he'd asked out Briony. He'd thought going out with her would make him forget how much he was starting to really like Eve. Instead, whenever he was with her, he kept mentally comparing her to Eve, and Eve always came out ahead, even though Briony was great.

'Thanks,' Eve said. She let her head drop forward, so he had more access to her shoulders and back. Luke continued his massage, imagining her silky skin beneath his fingers.

'Found it!' Jess cried.

'How to close the portal?' Eve spun round in her chair, Luke's hands falling free.

'Well, not exactly. But hopefully,' Jess said. 'I found Helena's diary. A whole bunch of them actually.' She held out a stack of brightly coloured journals of different sizes. 'I flipped through a few pages. There's definitely stuff about demons.'

'Let's take them with us,' Luke suggested. 'I'm going to get the rest of the stuff from the closet. You two make sure there's nothing else important around.'

'Story time.' Jess passed the diaries out when they were back at her house with everything they'd collected from Helena's.

Luke dropped down on the sofa and opened one with smiling butterflies on the front. The pages inside were filled with large, careful printing and a lot of crayon drawings. Helena had started keeping a diary young. He quickly flipped through the pages. One sentence caught his attention, sending a spike of horror through him: 'Mommy says I'm special.'

It was a normal thing for a little girl to write. But

did her mother mean that Helena was special the way most parents thought their kids were special? Or did Helena's mom mean that Helena was special because she'd have the power to open the portal one day?

He set the diary aside and opened a larger one, covered in slick neon green leather. 'You have to hear this,' Jess said, before he could start reading. She held up a diary with a googly-eyed kitten on the front. 'I think Helena wrote it in about the fifth grade. Listen. "I feel like a princess in a fairy tale. I can open a door to a hidden world. I wish there were fairies or pixies there instead of ugly demons. Mom says the demons won't ever hurt me or anybody in my family though."' Jess shook her head. 'Can you believe that, Eve?'

Her friend didn't answer. 'Eve?' Jess asked.

She slowly looked up from the journal she'd been reading. 'Sorry. I hardly heard you. This is the most recent diary. Helena got obsessed with demons. Obviously, right? Anyway, apparently the portal had to be opened on midsummer's eve. Helena wanted to do it herself, so she could be the one to let Malphas through. Let me read this part.'

She took a breath, and began. '"My mother refuses to turn over the responsibility to me, even though I know more about demons than she ever will. I told her I'd begun studying the dark arts on my own. I was trying to prove that I was the one who should honour the pact between Lord Medway and Malphas. I've even managed to raise a few minor demons. Only for a few minutes, but still. But Mom just freaked and had a fit, going on and on and on about how dangerous that was, and how it completely proved her point that I wasn't ready to go anywhere near the portal. She also said that even if she did think I was mature enough, it wouldn't matter. The power is only given to the oldest Medway descendant, and that was her, not me." '

'I wonder what Lord Medway got out of that pact she was talking about,' Luke said. 'Did he use demons to kill people who pissed him off too? Or did he get some other kind of pay-off?'

'Well, he was pretty rich,' Jess offered. 'You've seen the mansion. Imagine it back in the day.'

'What else is in there, Eve?' Luke asked. 'The most recent diary seems the most likely place to find what we need. She wrote it during the time the portal was opened.'

'And should have been closed,' Jess added.

Eve quickly scanned the pages. 'Oh, lovely. Here's a

rant about me and how I keep wearing slutty clothes to get Kyle to notice me.' She flipped a page and the diary began to tremble in her shaking fingers.

'What?' Luke asked, alarmed.

'I think . . . oh my God.'

'Eve?' Jess rushed over to the armchair where Eve sat. 'What is it?'

'I think Helena might have . . . might have killed her mother,' Eve choked out.

Jess gasped, her hand flying to her mouth. Luke felt a cold numbness seep through his body. Killed her own mother? Could she have been *that* evil?

'This part was written after the portal was opened,' Eve whispered. 'Helena's mother refused to let her even watch. Helena was furious.'

'Read it,' Jess urged.

'"I've been thinking about how only the oldest Medway descendant can control the portal and something yummy occurred to me,"' Eve read aloud. '"All it would take to become the oldest descendant is for Mommy to die. Why didn't I think of this before? I could have opened the portal!"'

Eve turned the page and continued. '"But no worries. Lord Medway made a pact with Malphas. Two of them, actually. That first one where he sold his soul for tons of money. And then the deal to get his soul back, the one about getting his descendants to open the portal every hundred years to allow Malphas and his demon minions to feed. Why couldn't I make my own pact? I'm sure Malphas would like more access to this world. And for more access he'll have to agree to do more than leave the family alone and return great-great-great-etc.'s soul. Much more. All I have to do is make sure my mother is no longer with us when it's time for the portal to close." '

Eve stopped reading and looked up. 'She talks about killing her mother like it's nothing. Like it's a little chore to be crossed off her to-do list before the date when the portal had to be closed. Listen to this part.' Eve took a breath and began to read again. ' "I'll just make Mommy a nice chopped salad. The roots of water hemlock will blend right in. HECATE11 said on her blog that it takes effect really fast and is native to North America." '

'She poisoned her own mother.' Jess covered her mouth with her palm.

'I don't want to say Helena got what she deserved,' Luke said, 'because nobody deserves what happened tonight.' He thought about the demons fighting for a taste of her blood. 'Nobody. But if you're willing to commit murder to have the chance to negotiate with a demon . . .' He shrugged.

'Every choice she made brought her closer to what happened tonight,' Jess commented.

'Was it even choice, really?' Eve asked. 'From what Helena wrote, Lord Medway made a pact that involved his family for ever. If I was the descendent of Lord Medway instead of the Deepdene Witch, would I—'

Luke refused to let her finish. 'No,' he told her. 'No way. Look at Helena's mom. She didn't use the power she had over demons to bring more evil into our world.'

'She didn't stop it either,' Jess said.

'Maybe she didn't know how. Why would she?' Eve asked. 'She was planning to close the portal. Maybe that's all she could do.'

'Helena must have instructions somewhere for how to shut it again.' Luke returned to his journal, skimming, ignoring everything that didn't have to do with the portal. It needed to be closed now. Before the hellhounds came back to this side and killed more people. Before some new demon came through.

'Nothing useful in mine,' he said about an hour later.

'Mine either.' Jess set down the journal she held.

'I only have a couple of pages to go in this, the most recent one.' Eve read in silence for a few minutes, then shook her head.

'Maybe it's something the Medways never wrote down,' Jess suggested. 'Maybe the information about the portal and the pact is passed down orally.'

'Makes sense,' Luke answered. 'It would be extremely dangerous to have the details written down. Anyone could find them.'

'But only a Medway could use the information,' Eve reminded him. She dropped the journal she held. 'Only a Medway. And Helena was the oldest descendant. We don't know if there even is another Medway. Maybe she was the last of them.' She raised her hand to her mouth, as if she didn't want to say the words that came next. 'Even if we do find out exactly how to close the portal, we won't be able to do it ourselves. We're not Medways. This is hopeless!'

Luke couldn't believe he hadn't thought of that immediately. But he guessed getting chased by demons from hell was an OK excuse for being distracted. He looked from Eve to Jess, saw desperation and despair on both their faces and felt those same emotions bubbling up inside him.

With the portal open, any demon that found it could come through. He thought of the pictures he'd taken from Helena's closet. One of those demons could appear in Deepdene tomorrow. One or all.

He tried to think of something to say, something to give them all a little hope. Finally it came to him. 'When I despair, I remember that all through history the ways of truth and love have always won.' It was the Gandhi quote he and Eve had recited together when she was battling Malphas. They'd found the line when they were researching a history paper. Who knew it was going to turn out to be his mantra?

'You're right. We can't give up,' Eve said.

'No way. We've kicked two varieties of demon butt. There's nothing we can't do,' Jess added.

'She's a cheerleader, you know.' Eve winked at Luke. He could tell she was faking her hopefulness a little. He was too. And Jess. But they were trying. That's all they could do.

'We'll find another way to close the portal.' Luke stood up, hoping what he'd said was true.

'What if the wargs can still come through even with Helena dead? They've been going back and forth. Feeding, then returning to the other side of the portal until they want to feed again. There's nothing stopping them from keeping on doing that.' Eve pointed out. 'How many more people will die before we figure out what to do?'

She's going to feel responsible for every person she doesn't save, Luke thought. He could hear it in her voice. Being the Deepdene Witch was an overwhelming burden. But she had him. She wasn't ever going to have to deal with the portal and whatever was on the other side alone.

The ringing phone pulled Eve out of a dream of the portal spewing an unending stream of demons. She answered with their hideous, gleeful faces still filling her vision.

'Are you juiced?'

'Luke?' Eve shook off the dream and looked at the clock. Five o'clock. In the a.m.

'Yep,' he said cheerfully. 'Do you think you've had enough time to recharge?'

'What happened? What's wrong?' She felt as if he'd thrown a pitcher of ice-water over her.

'Nothing, nothing, nothing,' Luke said quickly. 'I just have an idea about the portal. Can you meet me at the Medway mansion?'

Eve didn't answer for a moment. She traced one of

the cookies on her pyjama bottoms. Seeing the portal so soon after that creepy dream was the last thing she wanted to do. But she could feel her power deep in her belly. She was ready.

'Eve?'

'Just let me get dressed,' she told him.

'So what are we talking? Two . . . two and a half hours?' Luke teased.

'Half an hour, smart boy,' Eve told him. 'And you get to wake up Jess. Warning – if she hasn't had enough sleep she can be a little cranky.'

'We were fighting hellhounds yesterday,' Luke reminded her. 'I think I can deal with a cranky cheerleader. See you there.'

Eve hung up. She pulled on her favourite low-rise jeans and her black cashmere sweater with the peace sign studded on the back. Jess would think Eve was dressing for Luke again, and the fitted sweater *did* look good on her. But it was really that the peace sign felt lucky for a visit to the portal, and she had the feeling she was going to need all the luck she could get.

She started to put on her boots with the platform heels, but remembered how hard they'd been to run in the night Payne attacked her. Who knew if she might need to do some running again? Thinking of Payne brought feelings of sadness and regret. *I'm going to find a way to stop demons from using the portal,* she silently promised his spirit. *And I'm going to find a way to let the Order know that you died a hero, fighting demons to the end, sacrificing your life for Vic's.*

She put on her pewter-coloured high-tops and went downstairs. She debated whether or not to leave her parents a note and decided against it. They still didn't know that she and her friends had sneaked out of Jess's house last night, and if they ever discovered that their little girl had been out zapping a pack of hellhounds she would be grounded for the rest of her life.

Her parents wouldn't expect her up until around seven. She'd be home by then – she hoped. She grabbed Jess's jacket – they'd forgotten to switch back – and slipped out of the house. Luke was already at the Medway place when she arrived, standing outside the gate.

'Hi.' Eve stepped up beside him.

'You were right about Jess,' Luke said. 'I'm not even going to tell you what she said when she answered the phone. I'd blush if I did.'

'I'd like to see you blush,' Eve answered, then blushed a little herself as he grinned at her. She'd been flirting. Why was she flirting with him? Not a good idea. She didn't like the math. Falling for a player equalled getting your heart broken.

'So what's your idea on the portal?' she asked. Thinking about the portal to hell was definitely enough to suck any flirtiness out of her.

'It's hardly even an idea,' Luke admitted, 'but I was thinking about your powers and how they are getting exponentially stronger. Last month you couldn't set a piece of paper on fire. Yesterday one of your bolts snapped a pillar. I thought you should try zapping the portal.'

'What if I end up cracking the arch or something?' Eve asked. 'Everything on the other side could come rushing through.' Again her thoughts went to her dream. The demons had looked so happy as they came through the portal.

'Is that really different from the situation we have now? The portal's already open,' Luke said, his green eyes dark with worry. Then he smiled. 'Good morning, sunshine!' he called.

Eve followed his gaze and saw Jess rushing towards them. 'Sorry about what I said when I answered the phone,' Jess told Luke. 'It's just that I hardly got any sleep last night, and—'

'And that makes you a crankypants,' Luke finished for her. 'No worries. Eve gave me the heads-up.'

Jess narrowed her eyes at Eve in mock anger. 'Violation of the best-friend code,' she warned. 'So what are we doing?'

'Luke thought I should try using my power on the portal,' Eve answered.

'What will happen, do you think?' Jess asked.

'I don't know. Maybe she'll be able to close it. It seemed worth a try,' Luke said. He jammed his hands in his pockets. 'Easy for me to say. I don't have power. All I'm going to do is stand and watch. Well, watch with this in my hand.' He pulled Payne's sword free from the sheath under his coat. The blade glistened in the early-morning sunlight.

'You weren't standing and watching yesterday,' Eve reminded him. 'Neither of you were.' She walked towards the portal, Jess and Luke following her without hesitation. When she was about six paces away, she stopped. 'So just let fly, you think?' she asked, already focusing on the power inside her, feeling it blossom under her attention.

'Whatever feels right,' Luke answered.

'Remember your great-great-great-grandmother's diary entry,' Jess coached. 'She kept finding out new things she could do with her power. You will too. I bet closing the portal is going to be one of them.'

Eve raised her hands towards the portal and stared at it for a long moment. She felt the power surge, slide down her arms and out of her fingers. Instead of bolts, undulating waves of golden light were released.

'Beautiful,' she heard Jess whisper. She sounded very far away.

Jess's voice reminded Eve of how she had once put her hands on her friend and used her power to stop one of Jess's demon-induced nightmares. That night Eve's power had felt sort of the way it did now. Softer. Warm, but not scalding.

She closed the distance between herself and the arch, then put one hand on either side of it. Thin strands of the golden light criss-crossed the opening. This felt right. Eve slid her hands up and down the cold stone, and it warmed under her fingers as more and more strands of light filled the entrance to the portal.

Eve didn't take her hands off the arch until all the power was drained from her body. When she let go, the entrance to the portal looked as if a golden spider web had been spun in the centre of the arch. It glistened softly, then went out. 'It didn't work.' Eve felt hollow inside.

'I don't believe that,' Luke told her. 'Watching you do that – it was almost like being in church. I don't believe that nothing's changed.' He sheathed the sword, then strode up to the arch and tried to put his hand through. Golden sparks flew up, crackling. 'See. It's still there. It's kind of like you made a force field. It wouldn't let me through.'

'But what about demons?' Jess asked.

'I guess we'll have to wait and see.' Eve had given everything she had. There was nothing else to do.

Eve held up a slice of pizza, toasting Luke and Jess. 'To us.' They tapped their slices to hers. Their parents had agreed the three of them could go to Piscatelli's after school as long as they stayed together. They were supposed to walk to the rectory when they were done, and Jess's mom would pick Eve and Jess up from there.

They'd actually stopped at the rectory first so Luke could get the sword – just in case. Then, on the way back to the Main Street pizza place, they'd checked on the portal. The web, now invisible, had still sparked when it was touched, but it hadn't even been up for a whole day yet. Still, it had been a day without wargs.

Although they usually stay on the other side of the portal for at least a few days after they feed, Eve couldn't stop herself from thinking.

'The toast isn't good unless you eat a bite,' Luke told her.

Eve blinked, then took a bite of her pizza. She tried to concentrate on the perfect blend of flavours. For now, that was all that needed her attention. If something made it through the portal – well, she'd deal with that when it happened.

The smell of wood-smoke kept bringing her mind back to demons though. She knew it was coming from the sword, but her instincts connected the smell with danger.

'You'd better not spill on your new coat,' Jess warned Luke. 'Do you think we should make him a bib out of napkins?' she asked Eve.

'The point of the jacket was to make him less of a fashion victim,' Eve answered. 'A bib doesn't look good on anyone who isn't in a high chair.'

'I think he'd look good in anything.' A tall girl, probably a couple of years out of high school, with long hair down to the middle of her back, pulled up a chair from the next table and sat down with them. She reached over and straightened Luke's lapel, even though it didn't need it.

Eve looked from Jess to Luke. Did they know this chick? Because Eve definitely didn't. And she was pretty sure she'd rather not.

Luke slid right into player mode. 'You obviously have good taste, and that means you're welcome at my table any time,' he told the girl. *His* table? Eve managed not to snort.

'You don't know her?' Jess whispered.

'No, but I'd like to,' Luke mouthed in response.

Is he physically unable not to flirt? Eve wondered.

'Well, I don't know her,' Jess said. 'And I know everyone Eve knows, and Eve doesn't know her either.'

The girl picked up a slice of pizza from their pie and took a bite. Eve noticed she had those full lips that guys always loved. They were accentuated by dark lipstick. 'You don't know me, but I know you – Luke Thompson and Eve Evergold.' She didn't acknowledge Jess. 'You're the ones who found Payne's body.'

Eve dropped the rest of her slice back on her plate. 'You knew Payne?' The papers and TV reports hadn't mentioned his name. They'd said the body of the man in the woods, the latest victim of an animal attack, had been found without identification.

The girl put her pizza down too, and some of the cockiness slid away from her. 'He was my mentor,' she told them.

'You're from the Order?' Luke asked, eyes widening.

The girl raised her brows, an expression of shock quickly passing across her face. 'He told you . . . ?' She shook her head. 'We shouldn't talk here. Come outside. There's someone else who wants to meet you. Oh, and I'm Alanna, by the way.'

'I'm Jess,' Jess said pointedly. 'I was there the night Payne died too.'

'Sorry.' Alanna didn't sound particularly sorry. 'Your name wasn't mentioned on the news. That's how I heard about these two. It wasn't hard to track them down in a town this small. I asked a couple of people and, bingo, someone had seen them going into the pizza place.'

She stood up. 'You coming?'

Eve nodded. She still wasn't sure she wanted to know Alanna. But she needed to know more about the Order. Her brief encounter with Payne had shown her what it had been like to meet someone who understood in a deep way what her life was like now.

Alanna led the way outside. A sandy-haired man

about Payne's age waited for them on the sidewalk. He had deep lines in his forehead and carved around his mouth. Eve thought his grey eyes looked kind. 'This is Callum,' Alanna told them.

'Let's walk to the park I saw about a block from here,' Callum suggested. 'I think we could use a little privacy.'

They walked in silence down the street and into the park. Callum headed to a gazebo, which was partly shielded by willow trees. He took a seat on one of the benches inside. Eve and the others joined him.

'They know about the Order,' Alanna announced. The words came out in a rush, as if she'd hardly been able to keep them in until they'd found a spot where they could talk without anyone around.

'Willem must have trusted them then,' Callum said. He glanced from Luke to Jess to Eve. 'I'm surprised. He wasn't a man who trusted easily.'

'He . . . um, we had something in common,' Eve answered. This was her chance. 'We both fight demons. I want you to know that Payne died in battle. He was killed by a warg, but he managed to save a girl's life before he died.'

'Thank you for telling us,' Callum said.

'I'm still at the part where this girl claimed to fight

demons,' Alanna said, tossing her glossy hair over her shoulder.

'Would you explain that to us?' Callum asked. 'If you know about the Order, you know why I ask. Anything you can tell us might help save more lives.'

I already told them I'm a demon fighter, Eve thought. *What can it hurt for them to know more?* Besides, she had a lot of questions, and giving them information was probably a good way to get them to tell her what she wanted to know.

She started at the beginning, or almost at the beginning, with the day her fingers had given off sparks and melted her lipstick. She told them about Malphas, about Helena and the wargs, and about the portal and the web she had managed to create across it.

There was something about Callum, something in his face, that made her know there was nothing she could say that would shock him. It was a relief to spill out everything that had happened to an actual adult who might be able to give her some advice.

'I'm sorry we didn't know about the demon infestations in your town earlier,' Callum told Eve when she finally finished, 'and that we weren't here to protect you when your powers were so untried and you were so inexperienced.'

'We did all right,' Luke said.

'You did,' Callum agreed. 'You three did more than could reasonably have been expected of you.'

'And I kept Eve's hair mostly frizz-free,' Jess added.

'Ask them about the sword,' Alanna urged.

'That's a big reason why we've come. We wanted to claim Payne's body, and we really need to find his sword. It's very rare and powerful,' Callum said.

'Payne gave it to Luke,' Jess volunteered.

'Not possible,' Alanna snapped.

'Not lying,' Jess told her.

'It was really clear that it was Payne's dying wish for Luke to have it,' Eve added. 'It was like he wouldn't let himself die until he saw it strapped onto Luke's back.'

'He would have wanted me to have it,' Alanna said to Callum. 'You know that. I was his best student.'

'May I see it?' Callum asked Luke.

Luke pulled the sword out of the sheath he wore under his jacket and held the weapon out to Callum with both hands. 'It's yours,' Callum said. 'I can tell that by seeing it in your hands.'

Alanna uttered a little sound of protest. Callum shook his head at her. 'Keep it, Luke,' he said. 'You may have need of it again. I hope not, but it's possible.'

Alanna gave Luke a smile. 'It does look good on you. But, like I said, I think pretty much anything would.'

'We have to leave. We're expected back tonight,' Callum said.

'No! I have so much to ask you,' Eve protested.

'And there's much we would like to learn from you,' Callum answered. 'This won't be our last meeting. Before we go, would you be willing to give us a sample of your blood? It would be hugely valuable, and I think it would enable the Order to discover information about your powers that you would be interested in.'

Eve hesitated. She glanced from Jess to Luke, trying to decide from their expressions what they thought.

'I think it's a good idea,' Luke said. 'You have this amazing gift. Maybe the Order could even figure out how to replicate it.'

'It's possible,' Callum agreed. 'Imagine how much that would increase our abilities to fight the demons. Payne mentioned you also have the ability to smell them. He told me about you – though not your name – when he checked in.'

'They smell like wood-smoke,' Eve answered. She

could smell the odour now. *Just the sword*, she reassured herself. 'I guess it would be OK if you took some blood. Especially after what Payne did for us.'

'Thank you.' Callum pulled a small leather pouch from his pocket. He removed a syringe. Quickly and efficiently he used it to take a sample of Eve's blood. 'Thank you,' he said again. 'We must leave now, but keep in touch with us about any demon activity here or anything else you need. We'll help as much as we're able.' He handed Eve an embossed business card with a phone number and email address on it. That was it. No name even.

'I might have some questions, if that's OK,' Luke said. 'I want to put together a database of all the demon information we can use.'

'Of course,' Callum said. He gave a half-bow and then walked away, Alanna at his side.

Eve lightly rubbed the spot on her arm where the syringe had pierced her skin. It made sense to give the Order her blood. But it felt weird somehow to know that they would be examining it, drawing conclusions about her. It was almost too personal.

They're going to use it to find more ways to fight demons, Eve reassured herself. *That's a good thing, a really good thing.*

* * *

That Friday Eve and Jess sat side by side in the school auditorium. Huge blown-up pictures of Kyle, Ms Taylor and Helena were arranged on easels at the front of the room. 'Psycho girl,' Jess whispered, looking at Helena's smiling face as the principal talked about how wonderful she was, what an athlete, what an example of school spirit, what a good friend.

Eve couldn't stop staring at the pictures of Kyle and Ms Taylor. Their deaths had been so horrible, their lives stolen on the whim of a selfish girl who had access to astounding power. She looked over at Luke, sitting a few rows ahead with Briony. Was he thinking the same thing?

She returned her eyes to the front of the auditorium. Through the huge window she could see the autumn leaves whirling, caught in a gust of wind. *It'll be Thanksgiving soon*, she thought. *Then Christmas. The year is almost over.*

As the memorial service came to a close Principal Allison asked for a moment of silence. Eve closed her eyes and images of mangled bodies appeared. She took a breath and replaced them with the image of golden strands criss-crossing the portal. It brought her some peace. There'd been no new killings in the days since she put up what Luke called the force field, and Eve was hopeful that the web was strong enough to keep the hellhounds and everything else on the other side of the portal where they belonged.

Let the new year be wonderful, she thought. *Peaceful and happy and everything that's good.*

Jess put her hand on Eve's arm. 'Time to go.'

Eve opened her eyes and realized the auditorium had already started to clear. Luke and Briony had gone. Without even intending to, Eve found herself looking over at the places where they'd been sitting.

'Want to go to Ola's?' Jess asked as they walked out. They'd been given the rest of the day off again.

'Mmm . . . I don't know,' Eve said. Almost everyone would be over there, including Luke and Briony.

'We could ask Luke,' Jess said.

Eve looked up and spotted Luke waiting for them just outside the doors, and a weight she hadn't known she'd been carrying lightened.

'You OK?' he asked Eve. 'That was pretty intense.' He touched her arm, and it was almost like he had the same powers she did. His fingers sent what felt like glowing light into her.

'Yeah. I couldn't help thinking "what if" though.

What if I'd found out about the *wild animal* sooner—'

'You did everything you could possibly do,' Luke told her.

'Absolutely,' Jess agreed.

'So ice cream, coffee or shopping? What's it going to be for you two?' Luke asked.

'Undecided as yet,' Jess told him. 'What's your pleasure?'

Seth Schneider, Jess's long-time crush, who'd recently seemed to realize she was actually a girl and not an annoying little kid who was three years younger, stopped next to them. 'Are you guys going to Ola's?' he asked.

Jess gave Eve an oh-please-please look. 'Marcus is coming too,' Seth told Eve. 'The four of us can hang.'

Eve hesitated and glanced at Luke. He was looking over his shoulder. Halfway down the hall she saw Briony, clearly waiting for him. 'Sure,' she said to Seth. 'Sounds fun.'

Luke turned back to them with a jerk. Did he think he was the only one who had dating opportunities? She smiled at him. 'Looks like your girlfriend's ready to go.'

'She's not my girlfriend exactly,' Luke said, meeting her eyes.

'Why not?' Seth asked. 'She's hot.'

'Luke's not a one-girl kind of guy,' Eve answered for him.

'Depends on the girl,' he said, then started down the hall towards Briony. He paused after he'd taken a couple of steps and looked back at Eve. 'Some girls are more special than others.'

Look out for the next

Dark Touch story

Fever

Deepdene is swept by a contagious tropical disease and placed in lockdown.

And then teenagers start to disappear.

A demon is among them . . .

Coming soon.

Some angels are destined to fall.

Instant. Intense. Weirdly familiar . . .
The moment Luce looks at Daniel she knows she has never felt like this before. Except that she can't shake the feeling that she has. And with *him* – a boy she doesn't ever remember setting eyes on. Will her attempt to find out why enlighten her – or destroy her?

"This thriller is dark and romantic, an absolute blinder of a book. Every teenage girl (and her mum) is going to want to read it."
Sun

ISBN: 978 0 552 56173 0

A heroine who will steal your heart.
A house that will haunt you.
A love story that will leave you breathless.

Sylvie is broken.
Her father's death broke her heart.
Her mother's remarriage broke her spirit.
And a broken leg ended her career as a ballerina.

She's lost so much . . . is she losing her mind as well?

Shawn is the resident golden boy, the one everyone thinks Sylvie should be with, the obvious choice.

Rhys is handsome and mysterious and has a hold on Sylvie that she doesn't quite understand.

ISBN: 978 0 552 56135 8